JAY AND SILENT BOB'S

Blueprints for Destroying Everything

G

Gallery Books

New York

London

Toronto

Sydney

New Delhi

JAY AND SILENT BOB'S
Blueprints for Destroying Everything

Jason Mewes and Kevin Smith

Illustrated by Steve Stark

Gallery Books
A Division of Simon & Schuster, Inc.
1230 Avenue of the Americas
New York, NY 10020

This book is a work of fiction. Any references to historical events, real people, or real places are used fictitiously. Other names, characters, places, and events are products of the authors' imagination, and any resemblance to actual events or places or persons, living or dead, is entirely coincidental.

First Gallery Books trade paperback edition July 2014

GALLERY BOOKS and colophon are registered trademarks of Simon & Schuster, Inc.

For information about special discounts for bulk purchases, please contact Simon & Schuster Special Sales at 1-866-506-1949 or business@simonandschuster.com.

The Simon & Schuster Speakers Bureau can bring authors to your live event. For more information or to book an event contact the Simon & Schuster Speakers Bureau at 1-866-248-3049 or visit our website at www.simonspeakers.com.

Manufactured in the United States of America

10 9 8 7 6 5 4 3 2 1

Library of Congress Cataloging-in-Publication Data is available.

ISBN 978-1-4767-1422-6

ISBN 978-1-4767-1423-3 (ebook)

Normally, I would never steal a joke. Joke stealing is right up there with hobo killing: I refuse to do it, even if it is all the rage with hipsters.

Making a funny is a little like childbirth for the lazy and irresponsible: You have this idea that you nurture until just the right moment, then you release it into the world and encourage it till that whimsy grows up into at least a giggle-inducer, and maybe even a true laugh. You give a person a laugh, they'll deem you useful and keep you around forever, not kill you for sport and pleasure like you're one of those aforementioned hobos.

I was not the first person who thought to utilize a technical blueprint for comedic effect. I don't even know if it was Wile E. Coyote who led that first expedition into this little-used corner of the basement in the House of Ha-Ha's, but he was *my* role model for the blueprint gag. The goal-oriented desert dweller is known for his tenacity in trying to nab the Roadrunner, but the best part of their ongoing feud was always the schematics included in every Acme purchase the Coyote would make. The comedic setup was in the elaborate designs and how they were supposed to work, and the punch line came when Wile tried to implement his plan. Hilarity ensued.

Mine was a generation raised on Looney Tunes reruns, all of us alert and looking to the skies for falling anvils. So at age twenty-five, decades after my first exposure to the blueprint as a comedic device, I was penning the script for 1995's *Mallrats*. The characters of Jay and Silent Bob, first introduced in *Clerks* as local dope peddlers, returned for my sophomore outing. But a nervous studio exec cautioned, *Using two drug dealers as muscle for the hero will alienate our key demographic.*

Y'know—'cause high-schoolers just *hate* weed . . .

So, instead of showing them imbibing an Indica or sampling a Sativa, I was told to scale back on the THC in a few of the scenes, and make it a plot device. Weed would still appear in *Mallrats*— kinda—in the sequence when Jay and Bob knock out the first and second suitor on the *Truth or Date* game show with a phat, chronic blunt. The rest of the time, instead of being scumbag local pushers as they were in *Clerks,* Jay and Silent Bob became more benign—like cinematic dirt merchants who help save the day by happenstance, whether they're aware of it or not. But how to communicate mischief making without spilling over into marijuana-laced mayhem?

So there I am, writing the *Mallrats* script on my very first Mac laptop with the black and white screen, Twitter still a lifetime away. And I'm thinking, "What the fuck are Jay and Bob doing in the mall now, if not smoking and selling dimebags?" And that's when a childhood "wasted" in front of the television yielded a dull spark that would ultimately result in the book you're now holding, gentle reader! That's the moment I started thinking, "What if Jay and Silent Bob are working off Wile E. Coyote–kinds of blueprints to bring down the *Truth or Date* stage for Brodie and T.S.?"

Mallrats wasn't very successful at the box office or with critics, but a fan base slowly developed around it in the decade following the flick's release. And unlike me, those kids were raised on current, commercially-oriented kiddie fare like *Barney* and *G.I. Joe* cartoons—not the life lessons of the *Looney Tunes.* So, to them, *I* invented that blueprint joke.

Well, I didn't. I just co-opted it and stuck dirty words in it. Story of my life.

Now, nearly twenty years after *Mallrats* and the Silent Bob blueprints (originally drawn by producer Scott Mosier), Mister Mewes and I have joined forces with Steve Stark to take the idea of those silly schematics to a whole new level of stupid, applying the indigo etchings to lots of life's little lapses in logic and law. And we pissed ourselves giggling while doing it. It's shorter and sexier than that *50 Shades* book, so read it on the shitter or on the go!

But I strongly urge you not to try anything depicted in these blueprints in real life—and certainly not in the comfort of your own home . . .

Go to a friend's house. Let *them* clean up the mess you're gonna make.

—Kevin Smith

JAY AND SILENT BOB'S

Blueprints for
Destroying
Everything

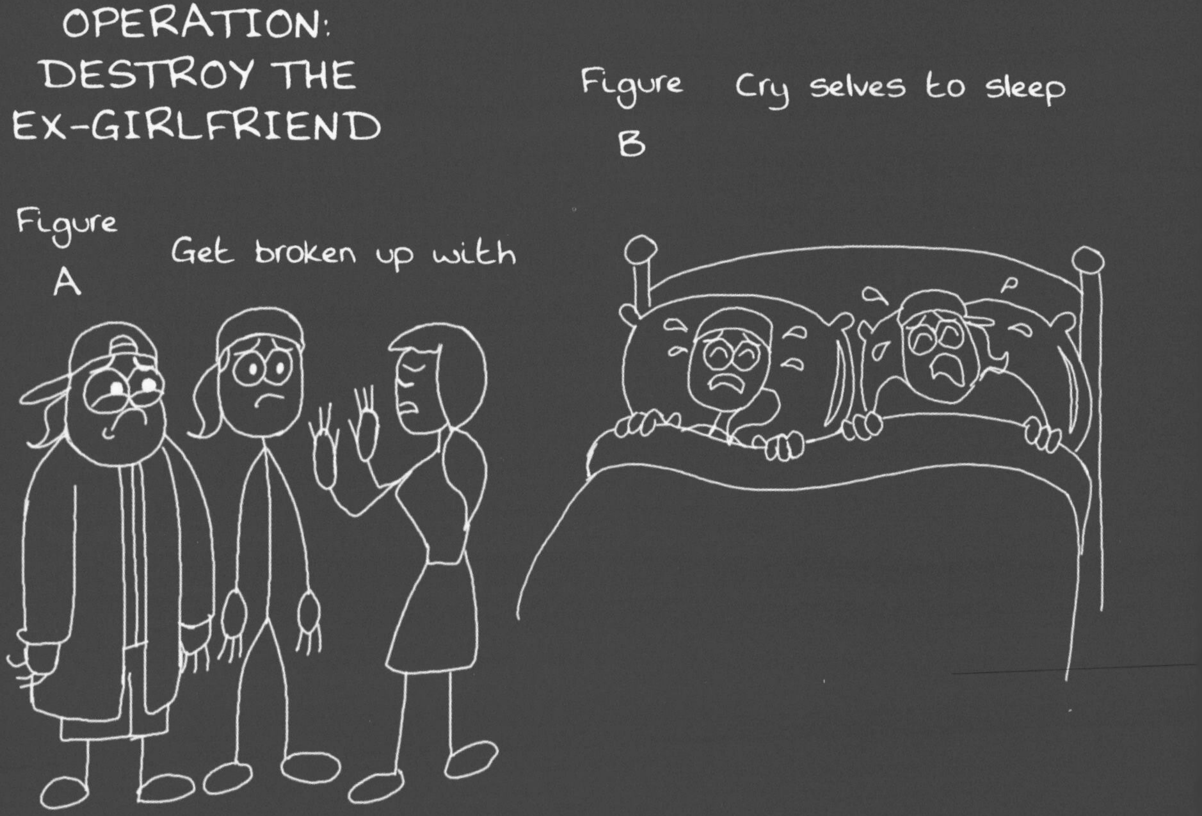
OPERATION:
DESTROY THE
EX-GIRLFRIEND
Figure A
Get broken up with
Figure B
Cry selves to sleep

Figure C
Explore alternative lifestyles

Figure D
Feel awkward

Figure E

Give women one
more try

OPERATION: DESTROY THE DEATH STAR WITHOUT KILLING THE INNOCENT CONTRACTORS

Figure A

Start a beat-off competition

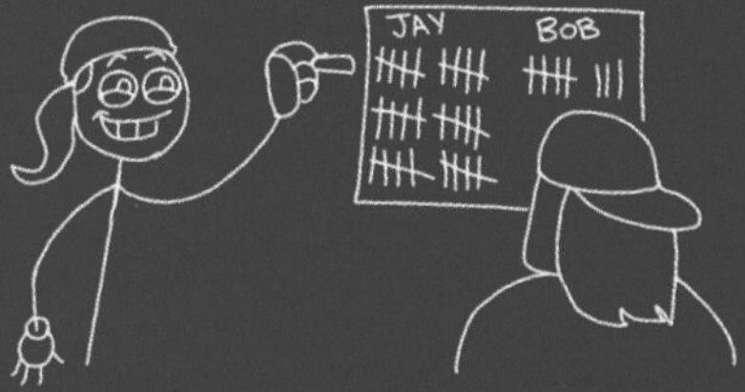
JAY
BOB

Figure B

Eight months later, accumulate a giant vat of semen

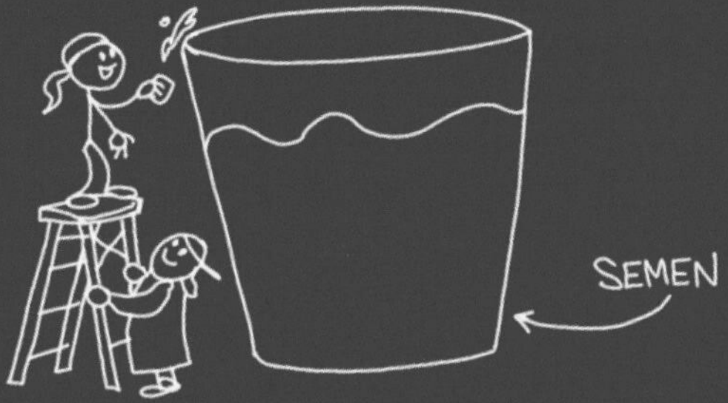
SEMEN

Figure C

Jay and Bob fly to the Death Star in a ship with bucket of cum

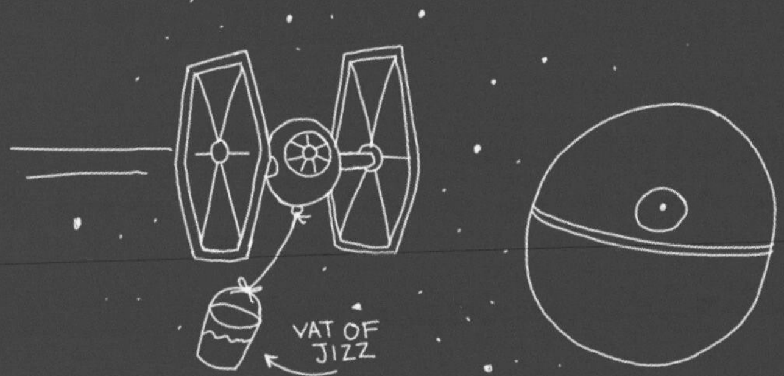
VAT OF JIZZ

Figure D

Launch bucket right into the Death Star's star hole

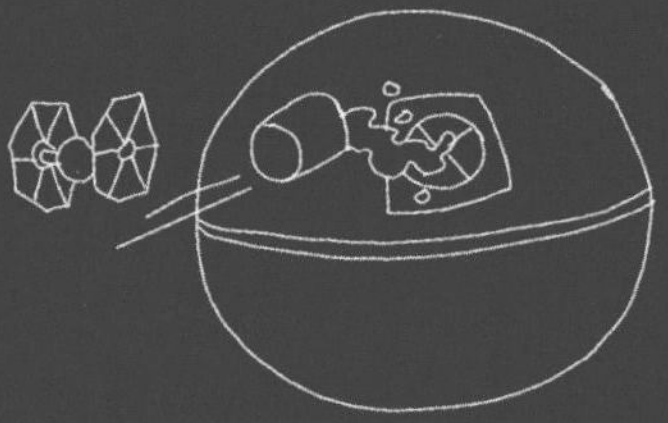

Figure E

Death Star controls become inactive from jizz

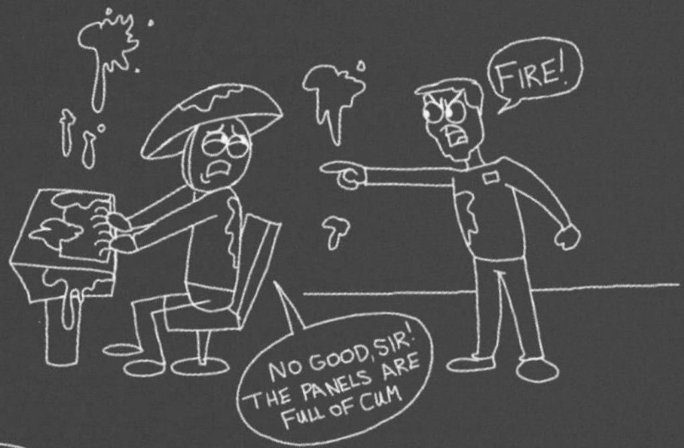
FIRE!
NO GOOD, SIR! THE PANELS ARE FULL OF CUM

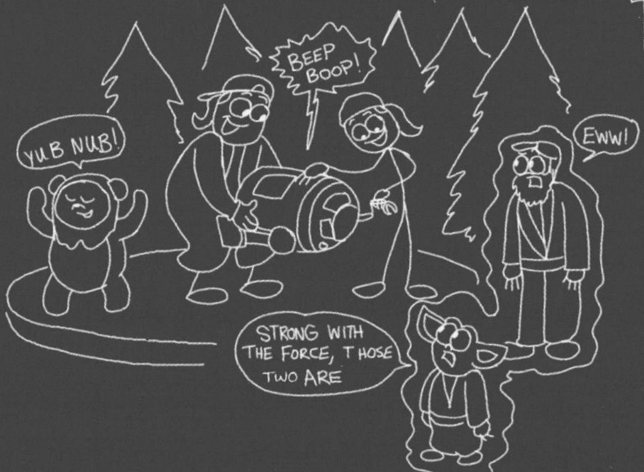
YUB NUB!
BEEP BOOP!
EWW!
STRONG WITH THE FORCE, THOSE TWO ARE

Figure F

Jay and Bob tag team a futuristic Fleshlight

OPERATION: DESTROY THE GLASS CEILING

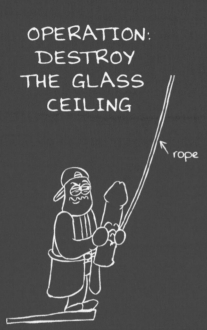

rope

Figure A
Get oversized novelty dildo

Figure B
Jam dildo up Richie Rich's corporate ass

Stupid bow tie

Glass ceiling

Women and minorities

He secretly loves it

Figure C

Let go of dildo

Figure D
Smile with victory

Jay has sex
with chick

Bob high-fives
minority

7

OPERATION: DESTROY MOOBY'S

Figure A

Get served piss and flies for the fifth time

MOOBY'S
MUNCH MUNCH

Figure B

Get mad

THIS AIN'T HALF BAD, BUT THIS SHIT'S GOTTA STOP!

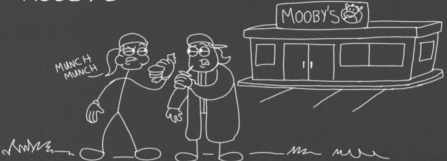

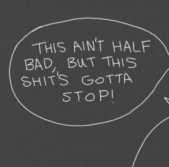

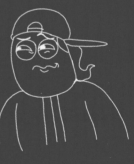

Figure C

Jay and Bob go to the manager and explain they're gonna take the corporation down!

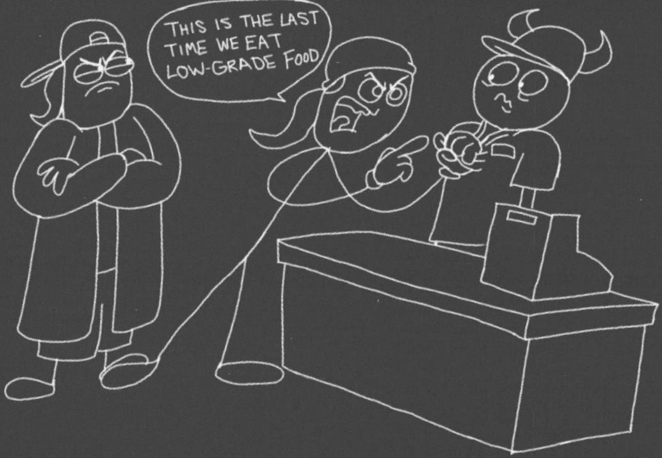
THIS IS THE LAST TIME WE EAT LOW-GRADE FOOD

Figure D

The manager apologizes and offers new meals on the house

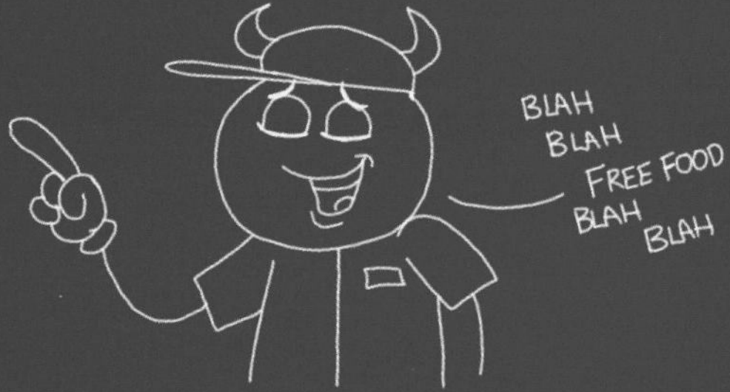
BLAH
BLAH
FREE FOOD
BLAH
BLAH

Figure E

Ponder the proposal...

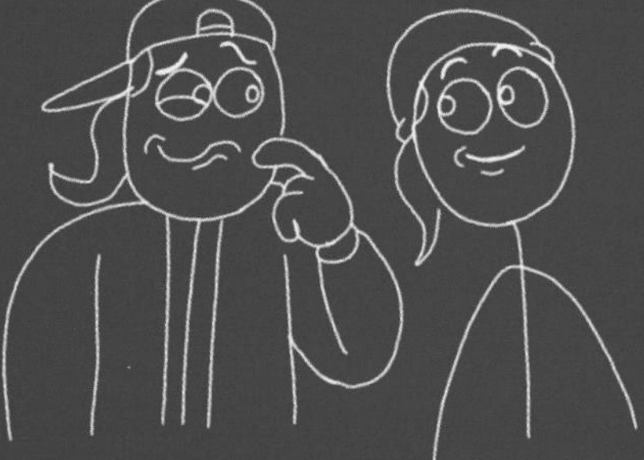

See figure A, repeat

OPERATION: DESTROY EVIDENCE OF ONLINE PERVERSION

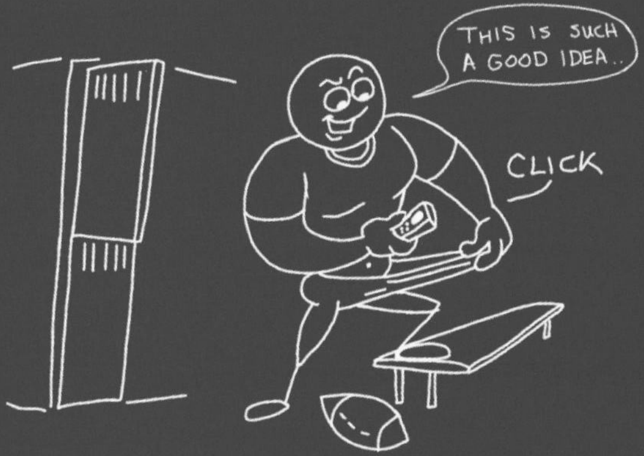
THIS IS SUCH A GOOD IDEA..
CLICK

Figure A

Famous football quarterback takes picture of his cock and sends it to a reporter

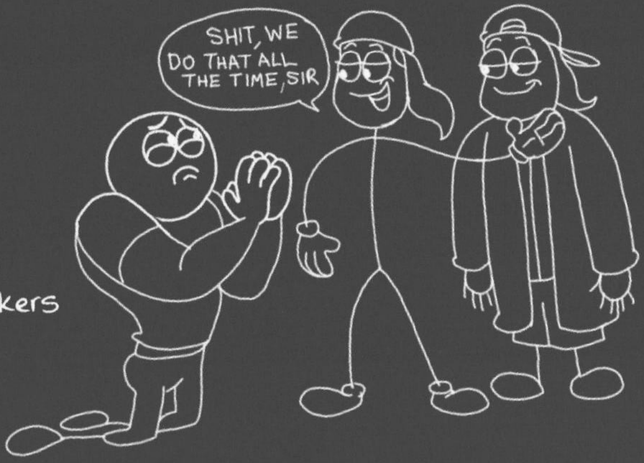
SHIT, WE DO THAT ALL THE TIME, SIR

Figure B

He gets in shit and calls in the help of us suave motherfuckers

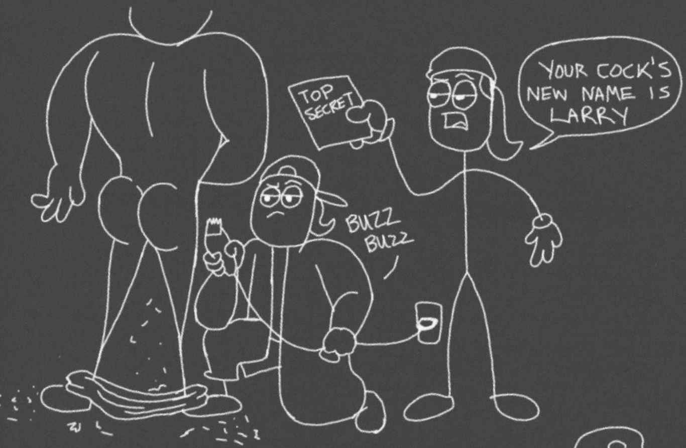
TOP SECRET
YOUR COCK'S NEW NAME IS LARRY
BUZZ BUZZ

Figure C

Jay and Bob give his cock a new identity, hairstyle, and life in a new state

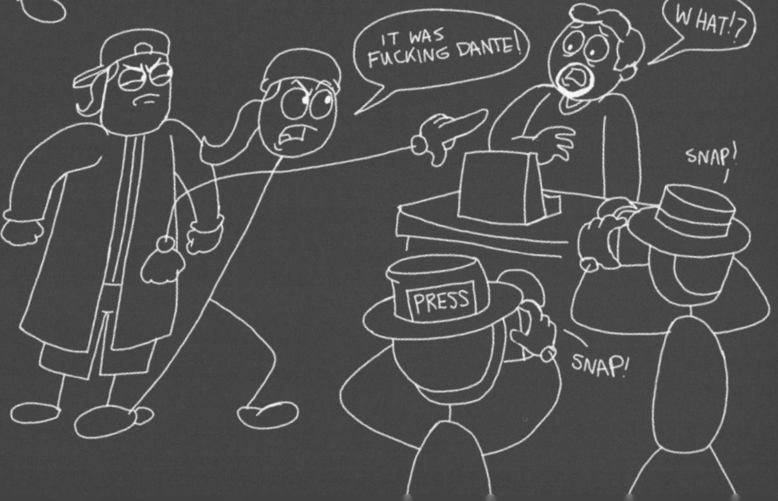
IT WAS FUCKING DANTE!
WHAT!?
SNAP!
PRESS
SNAP!

Figure D

Blame the pics on some other cock

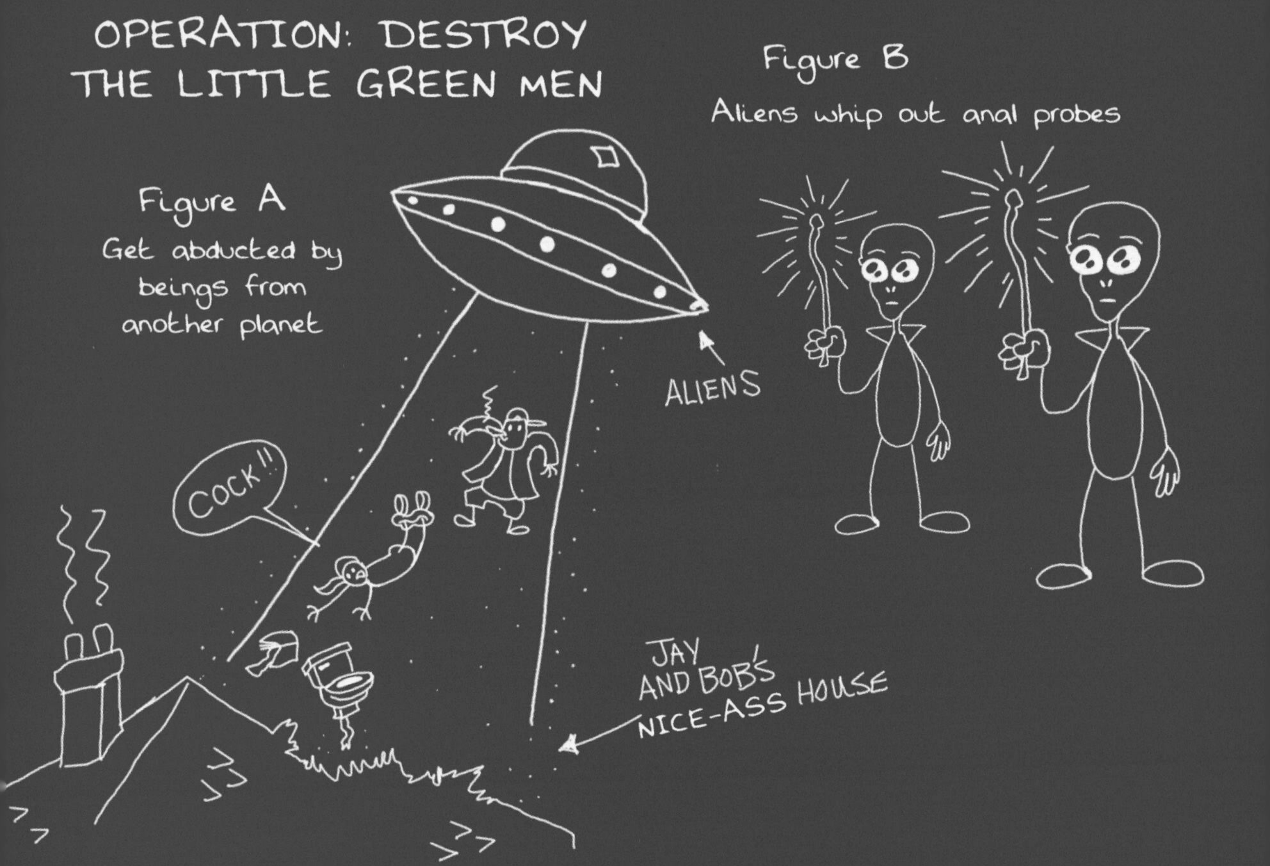
OPERATION: DESTROY
THE LITTLE GREEN MEN
Figure A
Get abducted by beings from another planet
Figure B
Aliens whip out anal probes
ALIENS
COCK!!
JAY AND BOB'S NICE-ASS HOUSE

Figure C

Where most humans would break, Jay and Bob outlast the probing for days

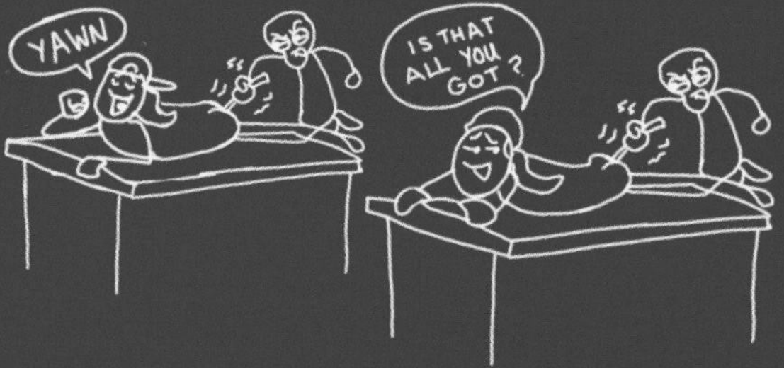
YAWN
IS THAT ALL YOU GOT?

Figure D

Aliens are in disbelief

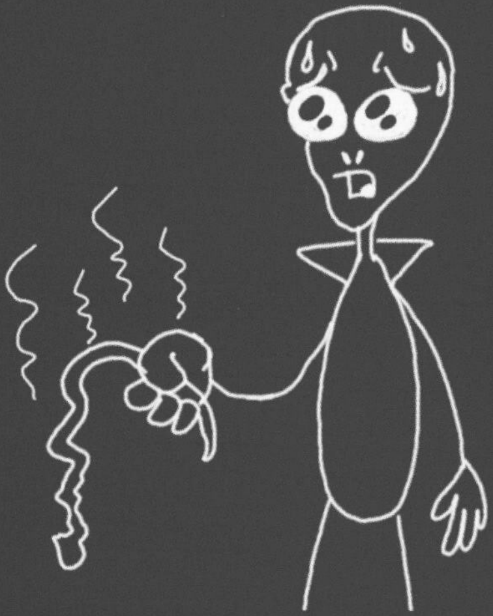

Figure E

Awesome humans are crowned their kings

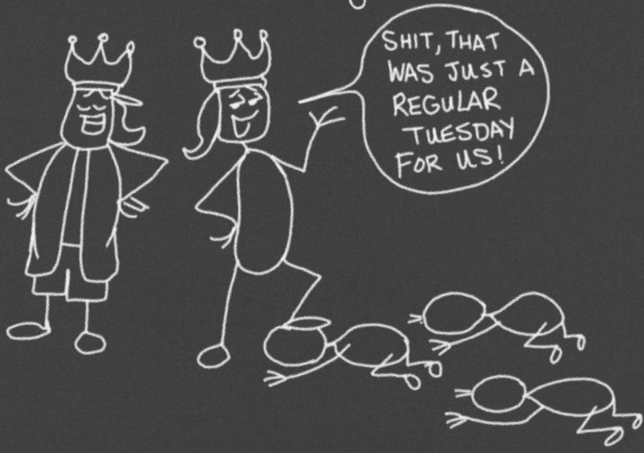
SHIT, THAT WAS JUST A REGULAR TUESDAY FOR US!

OPERATION: DESTROY A FRIENDSHIP

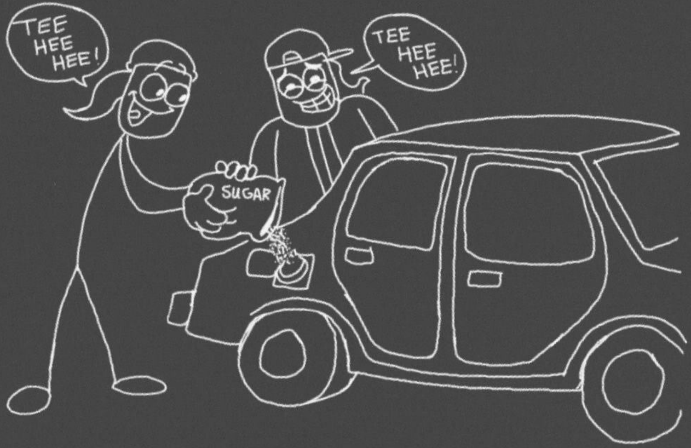
TEE HEE HEE!
TEE HEE HEE!
SUGAR

Figure A

Pour sugar in his gas tank

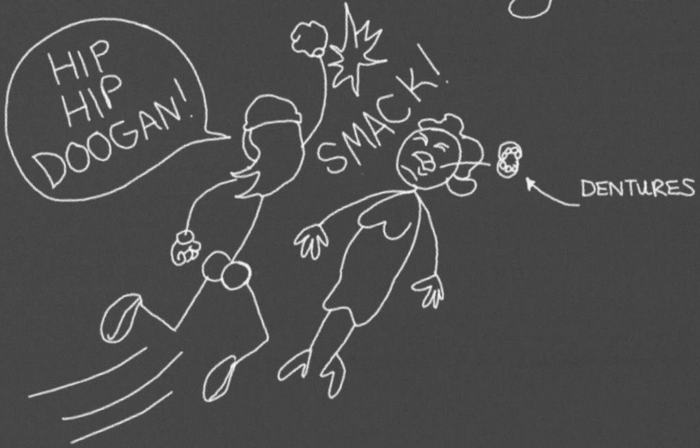
HIP HIP DOOGAN!
SMACK!
DENTURES

Figure B

Uppercut his grandma

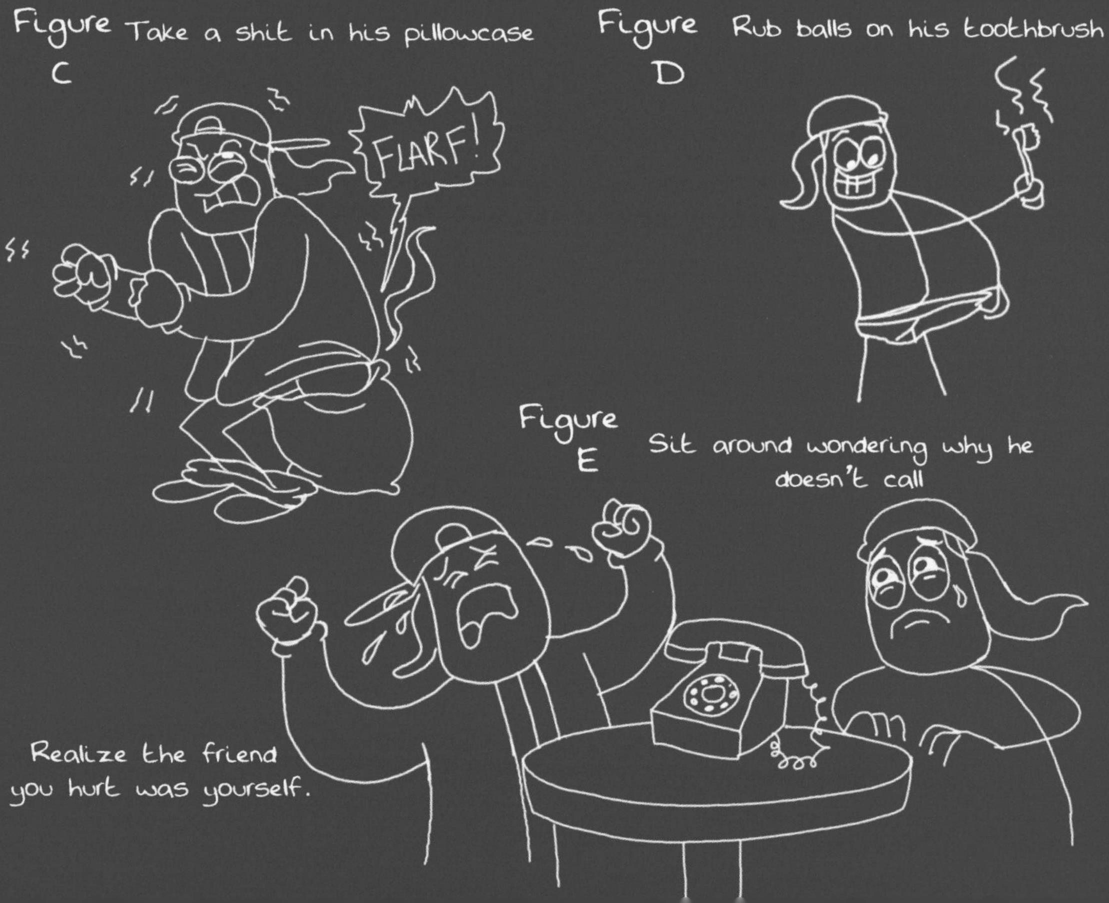
Figure C Take a shit in his pillowcase
FLARF!
Figure D Rub balls on his toothbrush
Figure E Sit around wondering why he doesn't call
Realize the friend you hurt was yourself.

OPERATION: DESTROY LIAM NEESON'S COCK

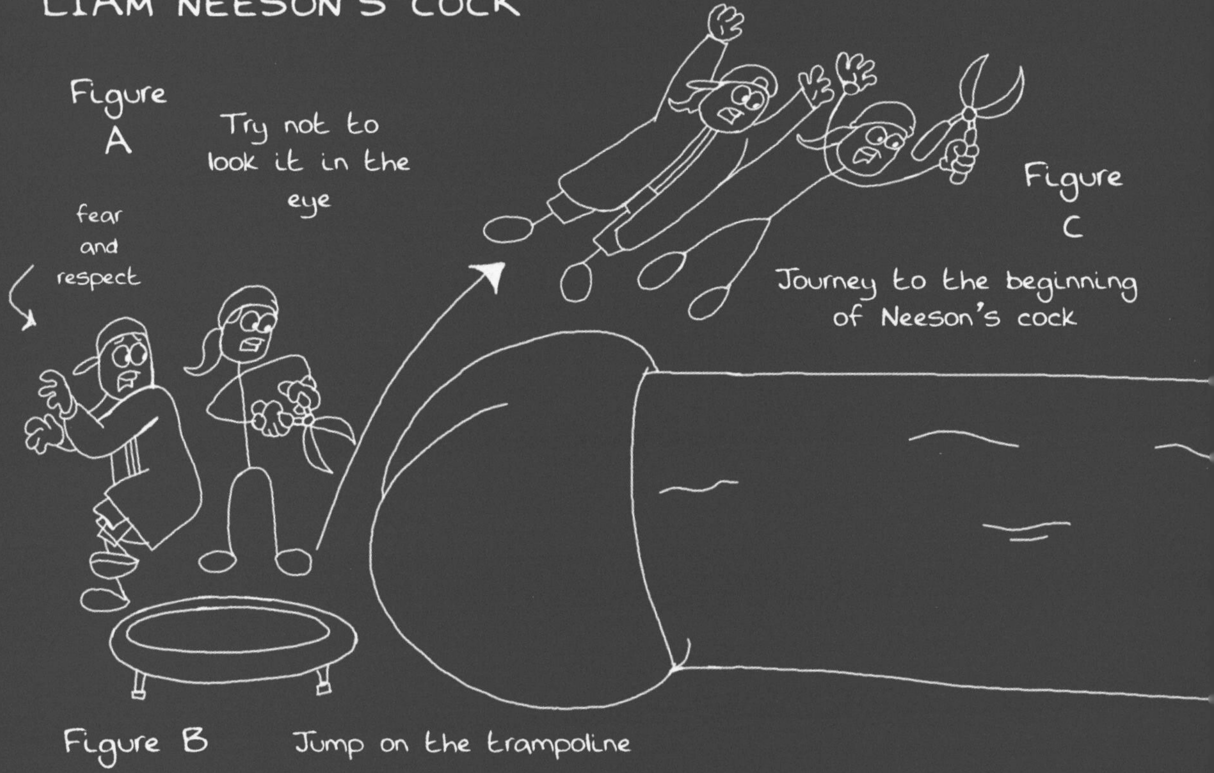
Figure A
Try not to look it in the eye
fear and respect
Figure B
Jump on the trampoline
Figure C
Journey to the beginning of Neeson's cock

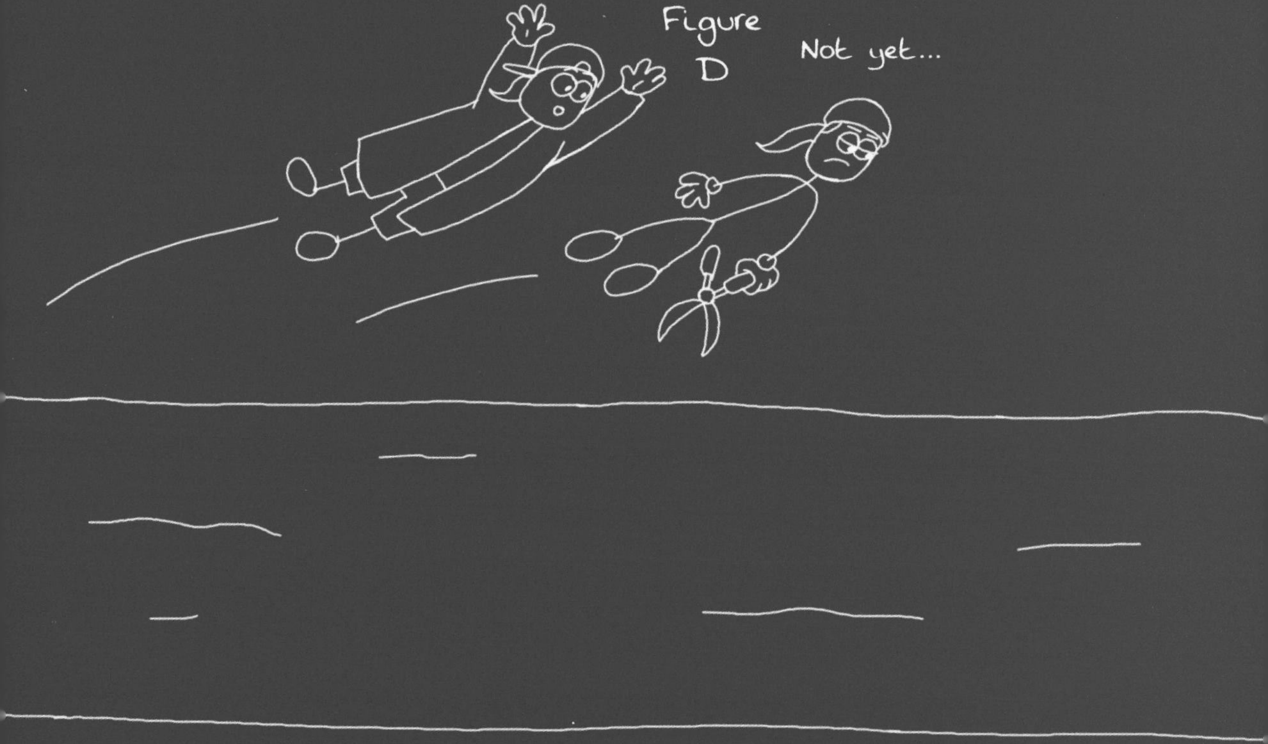
Figure
D
Not yet...

OPERATION: DESTROY LIAM NEESON'S COCK (CONT'D)

Figure E

A little more.....

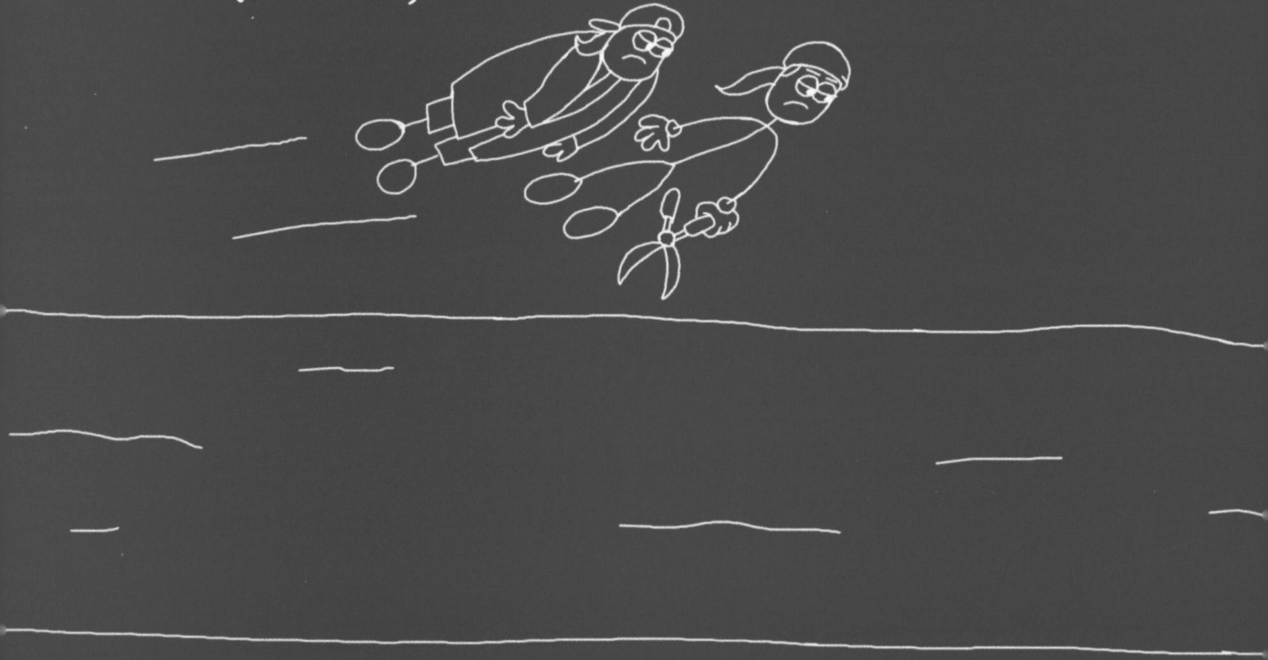

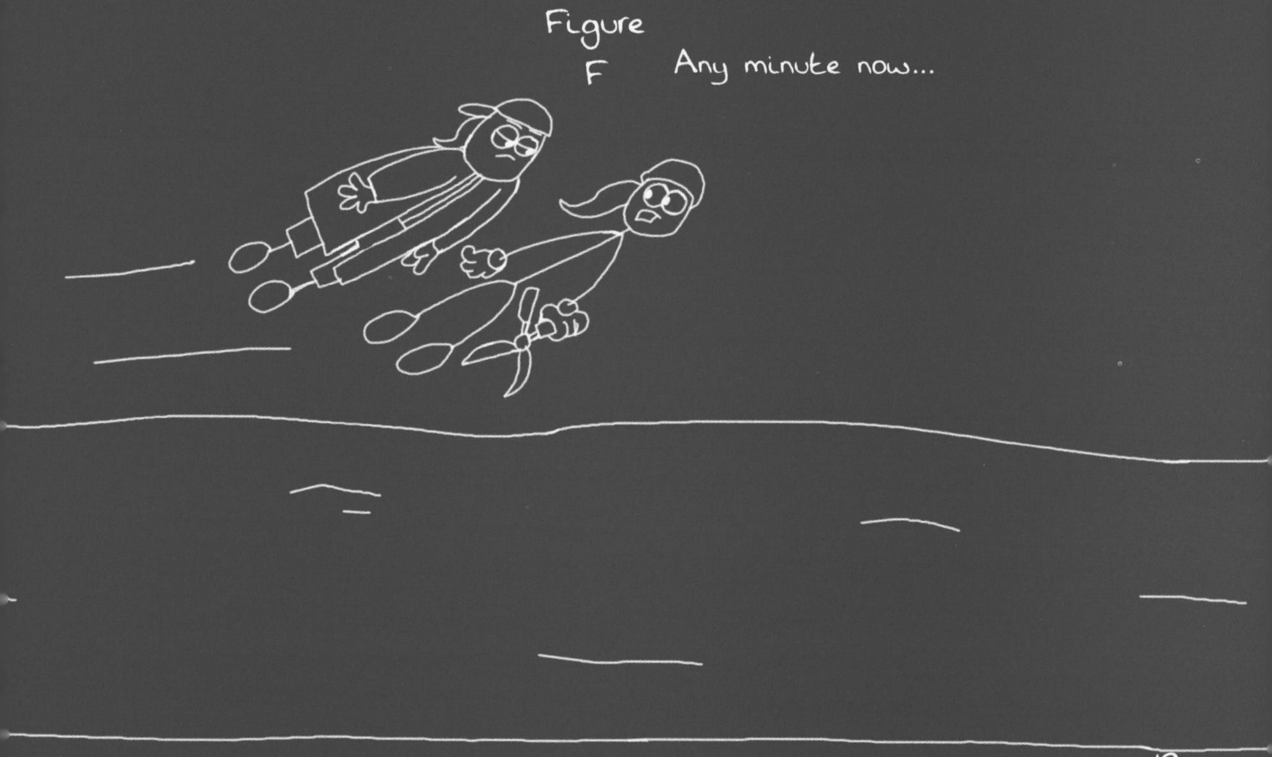
Figure
F
Any minute now...

OPERATION: DESTROY LIAM NEESON'S COCK (CONT'D)

Figure G

Getting closer......

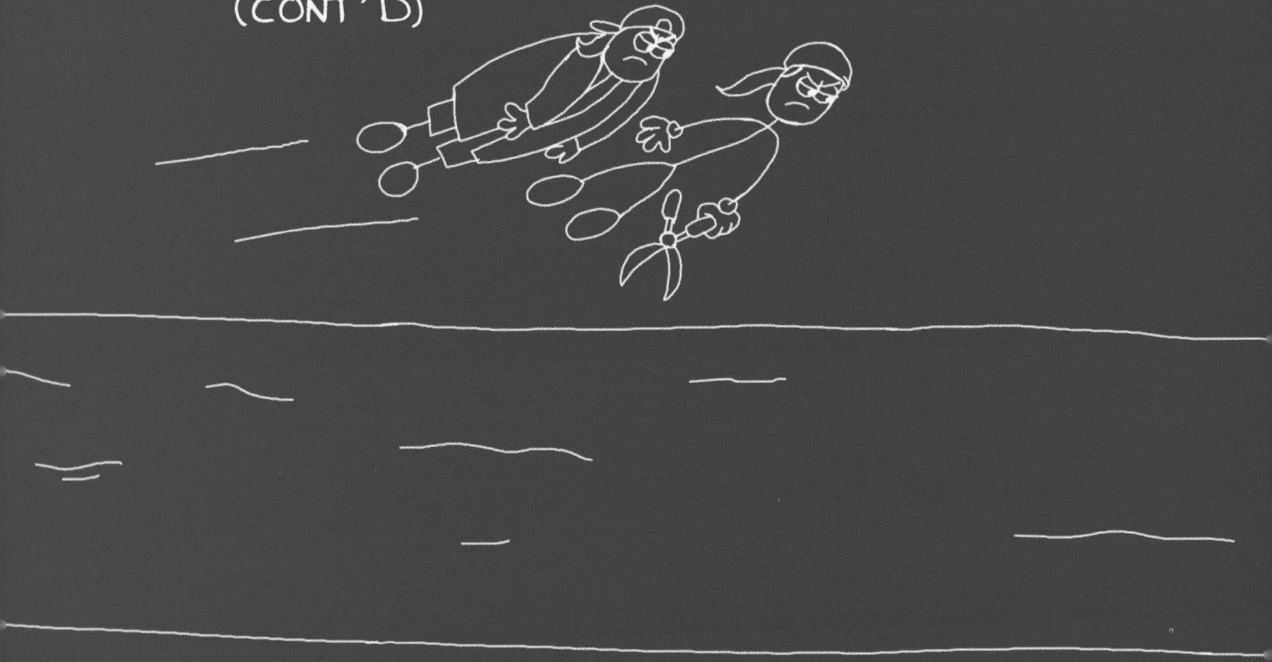

Figure H

Run out of air time

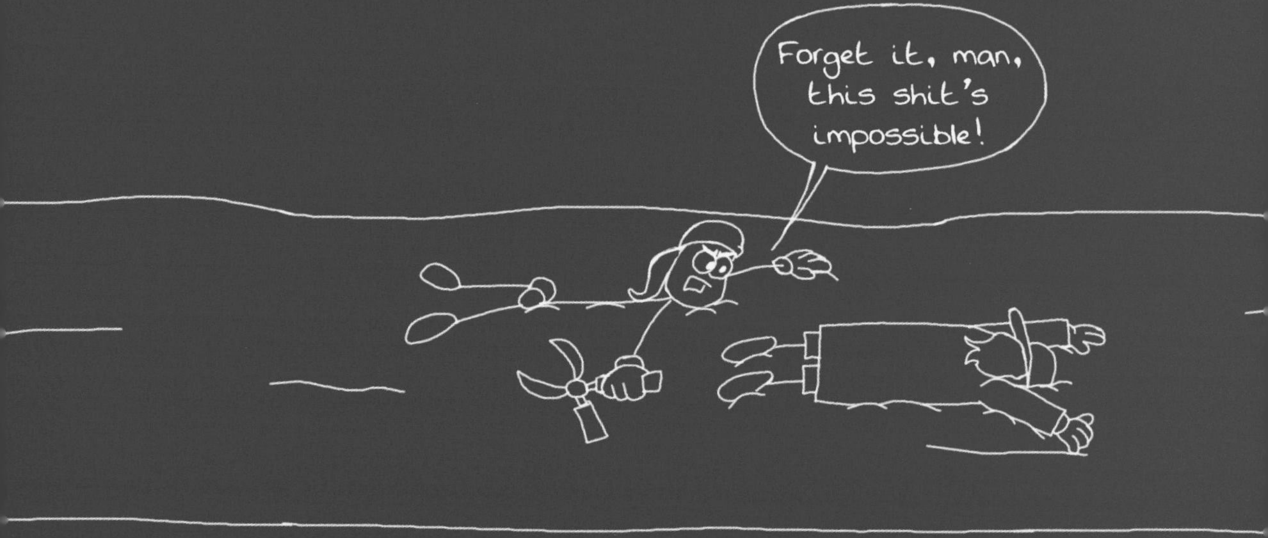

OPERATION: DESTROY CAPTAIN CHUFFA

Figure A

Jay and Bob's nemesis, Captain Chuffa, is ruining movies

CHUFFA! CHUFFA!

SCREEN-WRITER

CPT. CHUFFA

Figure B

Remind him how lucky he is to win the lottery of life by getting to make movies

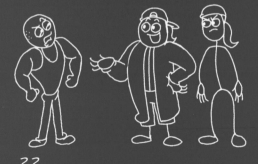

Figure C

If simple human approach cannot penetrate years of First World pampering...

HIT ME!

22

Figure D

Yippie-kay-yay that spoiled dick

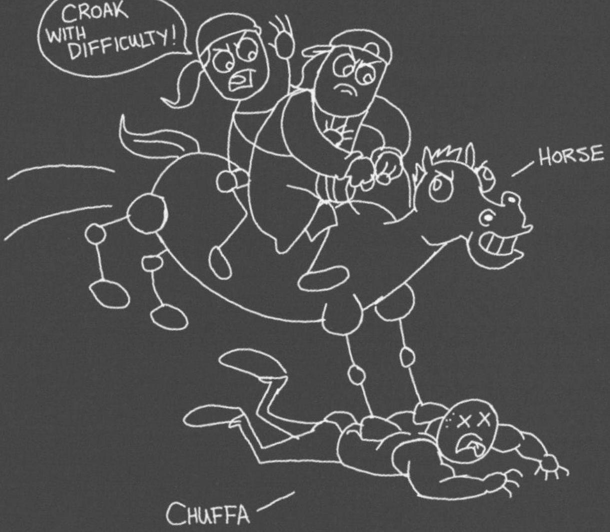

CROAK WITH DIFFICULTY!
HORSE
CHUFFA

Figure E

Get invited to Hollywood threesome with thankful lady studio exec!

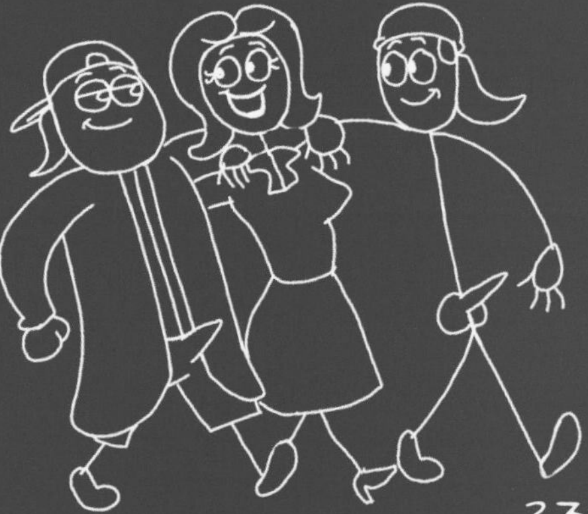

OPERATION:
DESTROY SELF-DOUBT

Figure
A

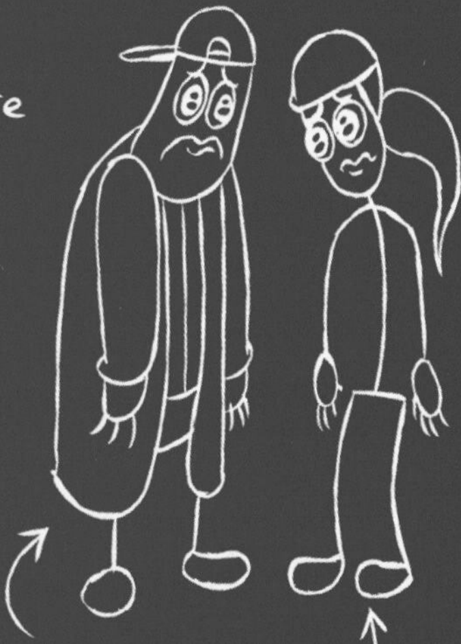

Jay and Bob
all doubtful
and shit

Figure B
Remember that
they sell weed

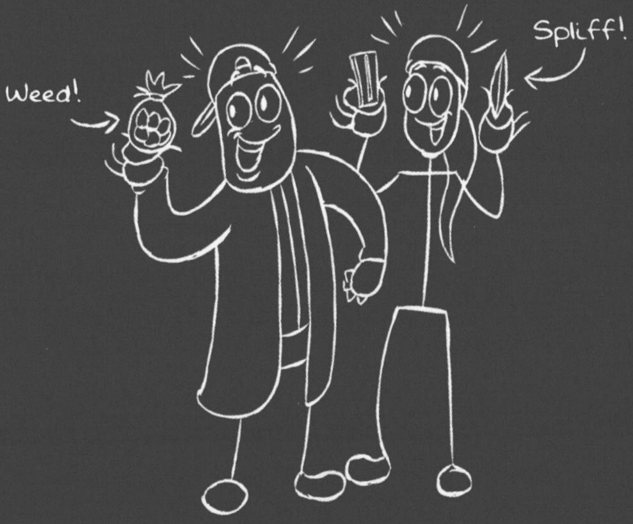
Weed!
Spliff!

Figure
C

Vigorously smoke weed

Figure
D

Doubt gone

25

OPERATION: DESTROY POVERTY

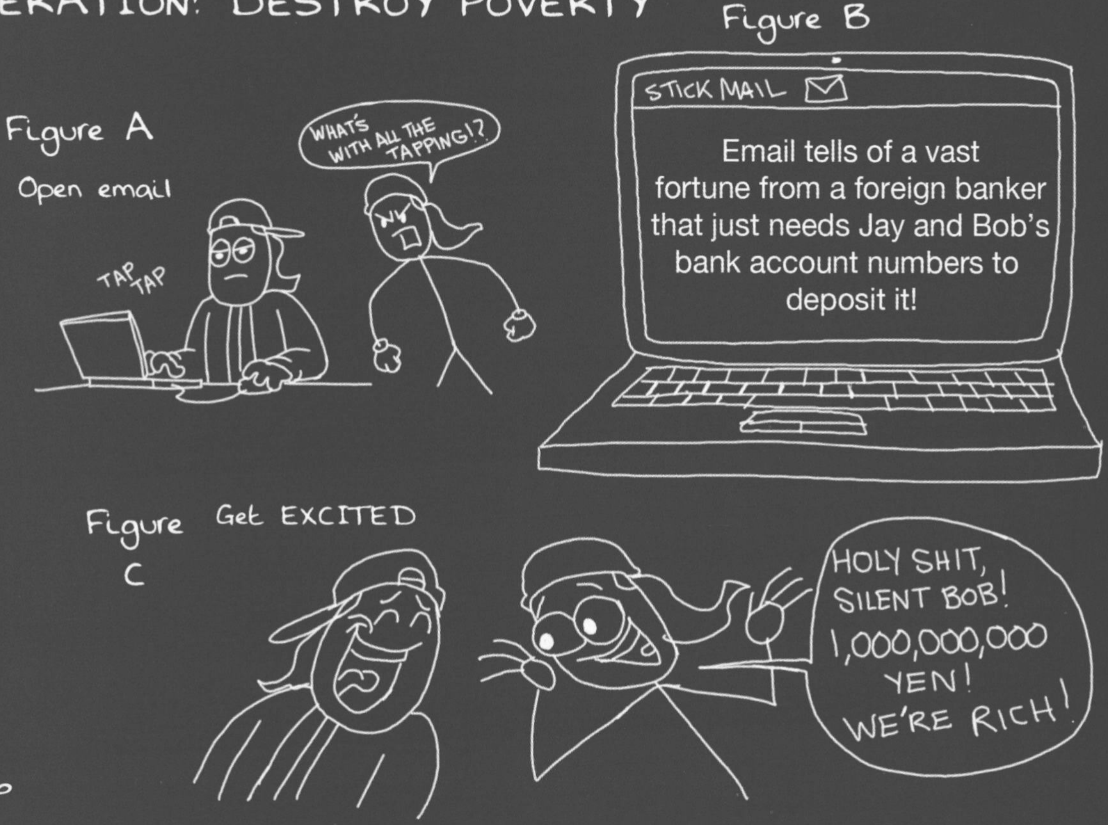
Figure B
STICK MAIL
Email tells of a vast fortune from a foreign banker that just needs Jay and Bob's bank account numbers to deposit it!
Figure A
Open email
WHAT'S WITH ALL THE TAPPING!?
TAP TAP
Figure C
Get EXCITED
HOLY SHIT, SILENT BOB! 1,000,000,000 YEN! WE'RE RICH!

Figure C

Send bank account numbers

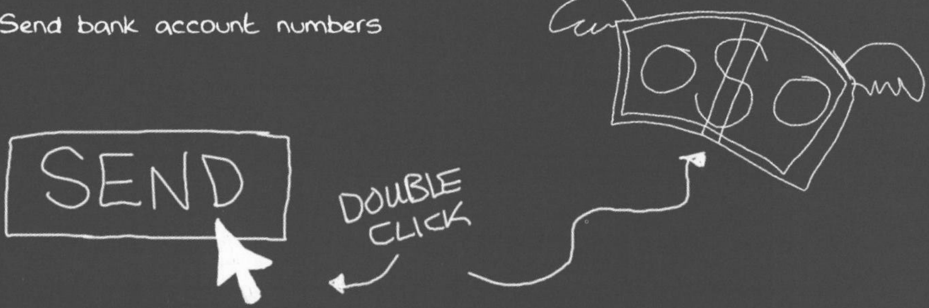
SEND
DOUBLE CLICK

Figure D

Bank accounts are robbed dry – realize someone else's poverty just got solved

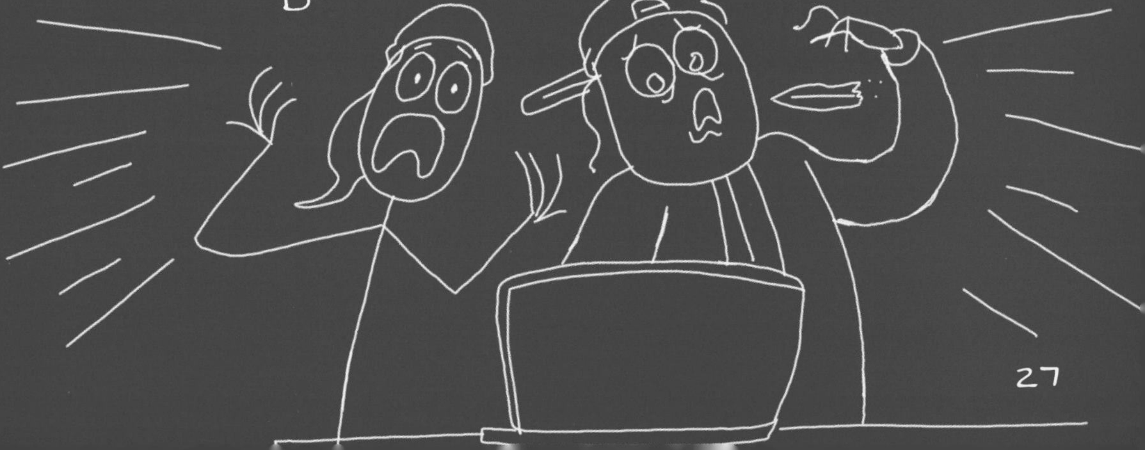

OPERATION: DESTROY THE HUNGER GAMES

Figure A
Before the bow-and-arrow girl can volunteer for her sister...

Figure B
Jay and Bob interrupt the ceremony

Figure C

And show them BATTLE ROYALE

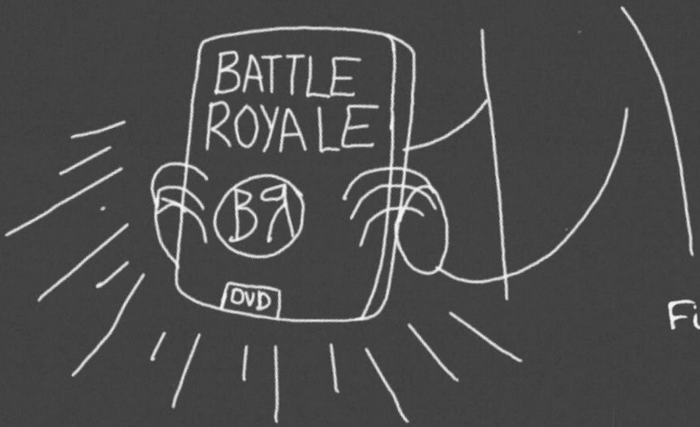
BATTLE ROYALE
BR
DVD

Figure E

Jay and Bob leave their fucked-up world even more disillusioned

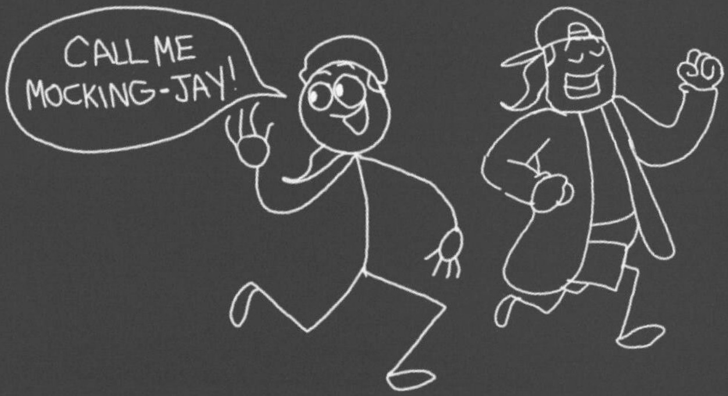
CALL ME MOCKING-JAY!

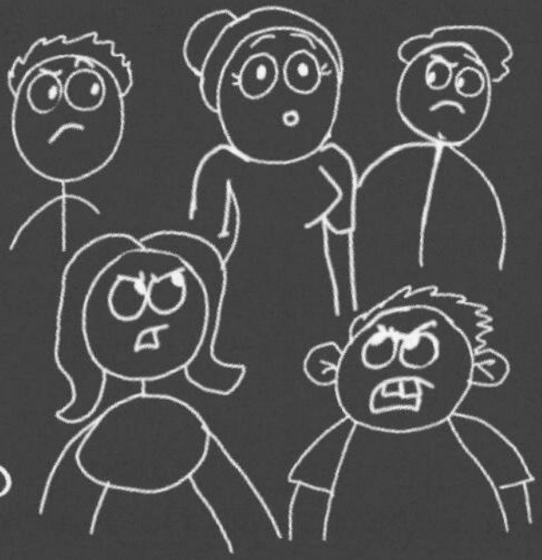

Figure D

The crowd realizes it's all been done before

OPERATION: DESTROY EXTRA POUNDS

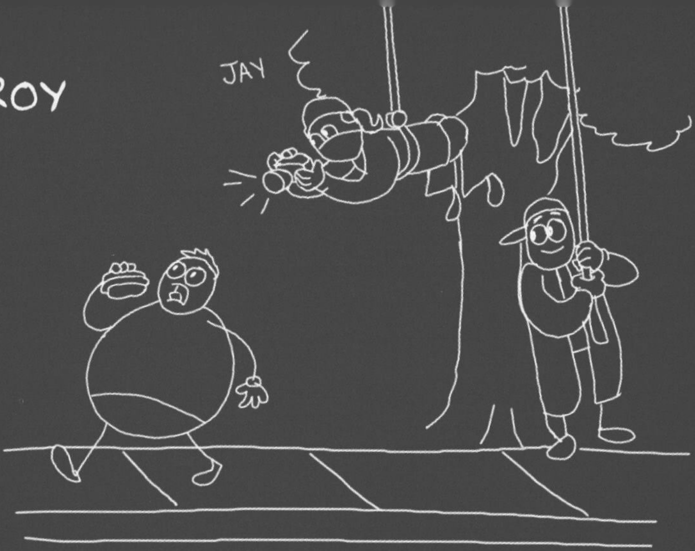
JAY

Figure A

Database everyone who is overweight and over 18

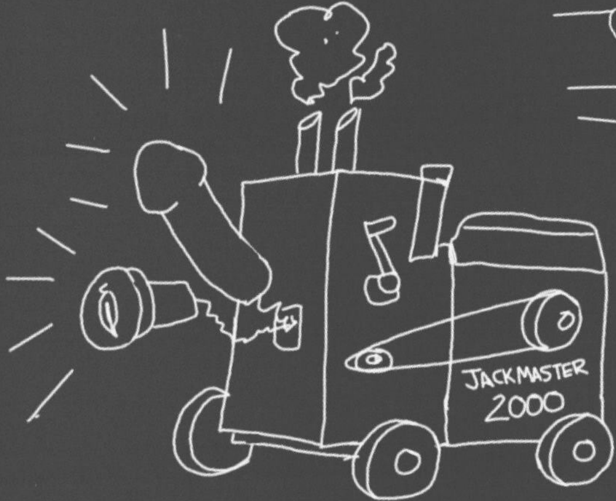
JACKMASTER 2000

Figure B

Realizing that sex burns nearly 1,000,000 calories, create a massive fuck machine

Figure C Send it as a secret gift to all people on the database

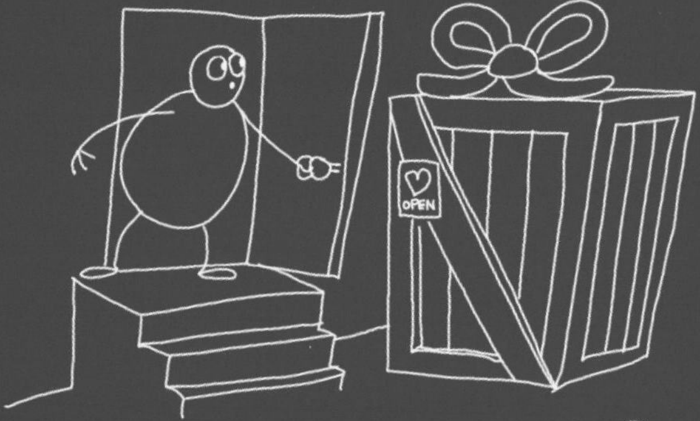
OPEN

Figure D They get the extra pounds fucked out of them

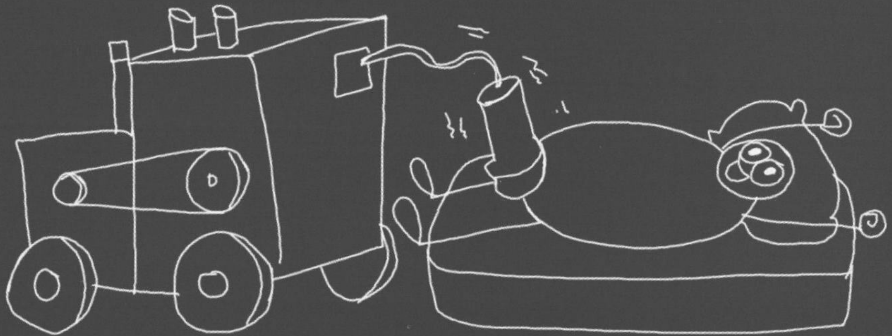

OPERATION: DESTROY THE FEAR OF YOUR OWN DEMISE

Figure A

Realize one day you will die

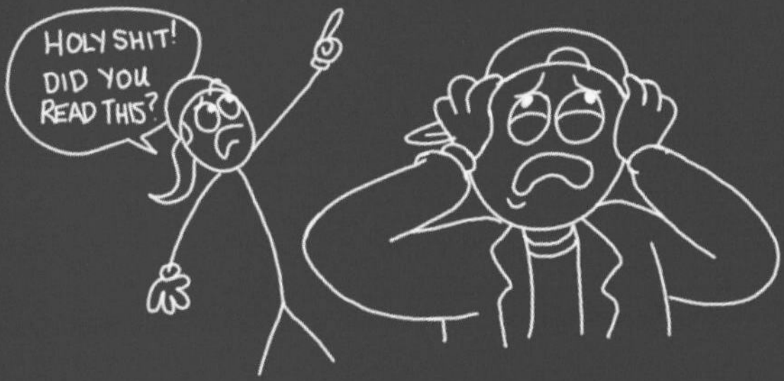
HOLY SHIT! DID YOU READ THIS?

Figure B

Put on a helmet

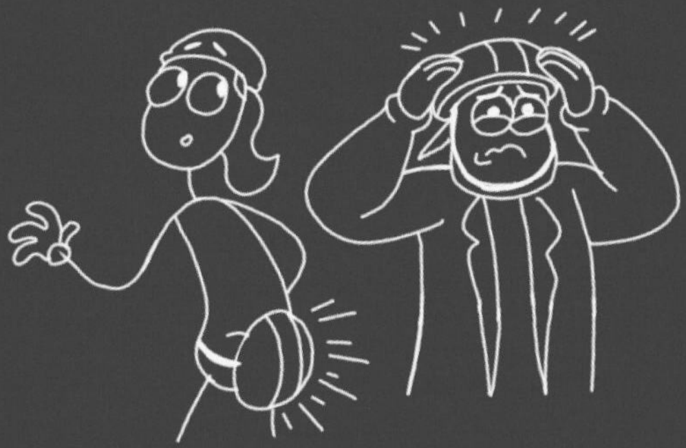

Figure C

Put on body armor

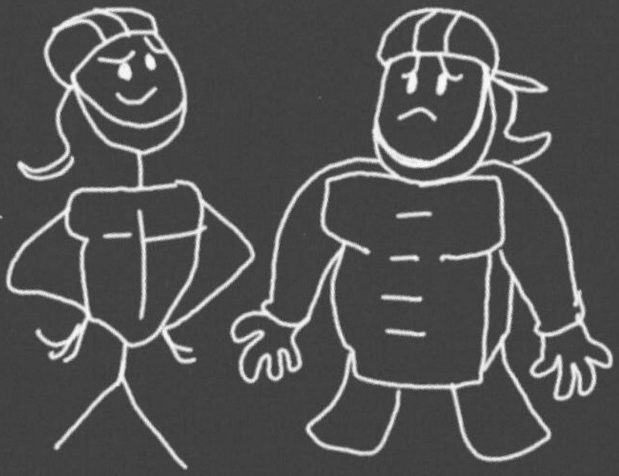

Figure D

Wrap entire body in thick bubble wrap

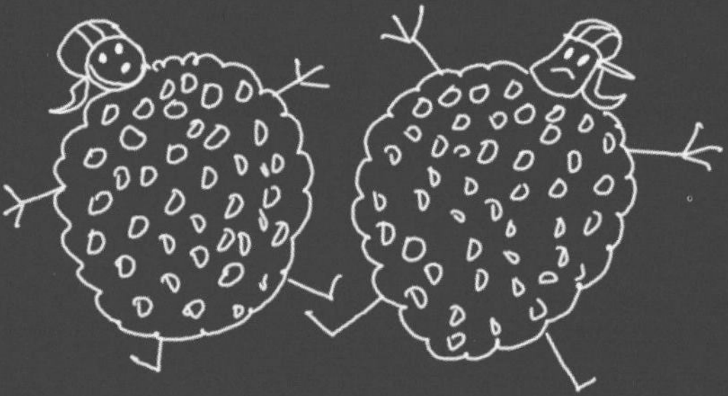

Punch Death in his stupid turkey neck!!

Figure E

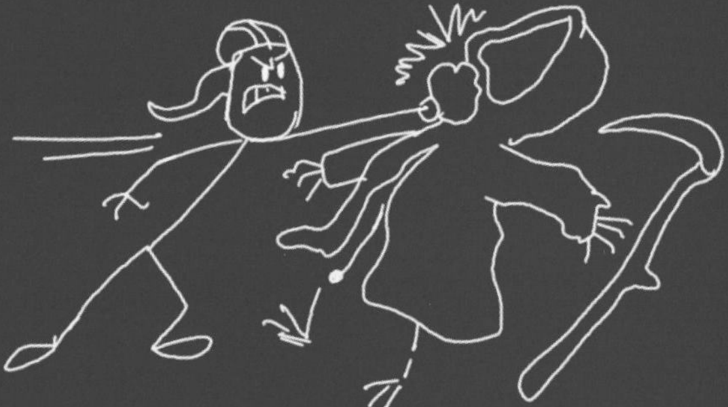

Figure F

Live forever

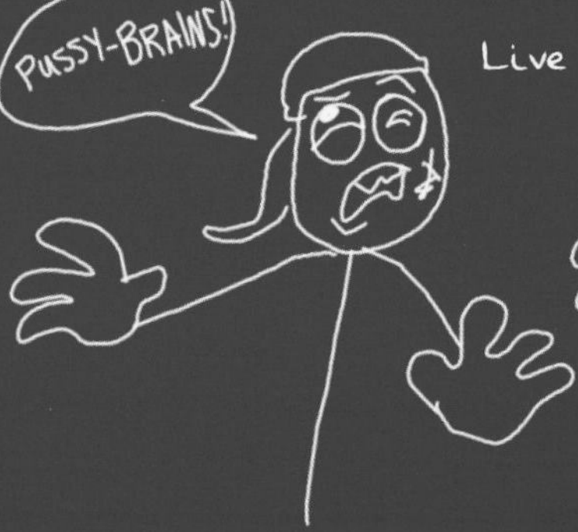

PUSSY-BRAINS!

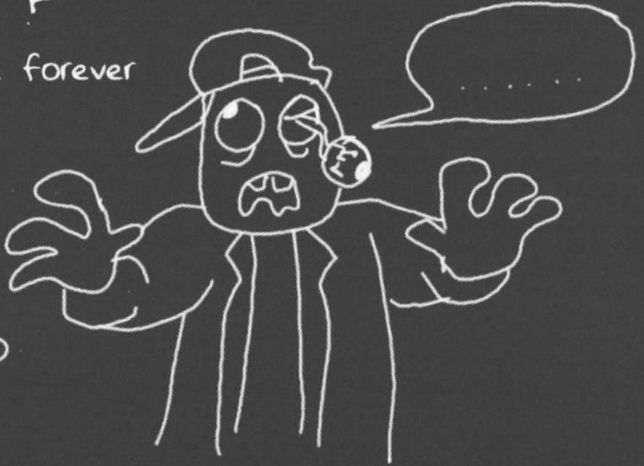

OPERATION: DESTROY THE MONSTER THAT EATS COOKIES

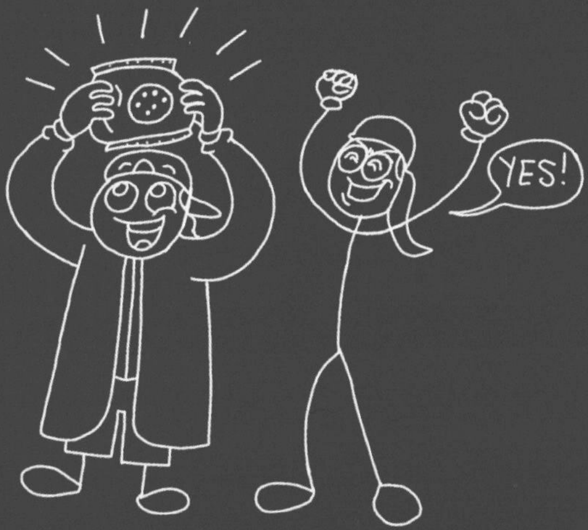
YES!

Figure A

Purchase a bag of cookies

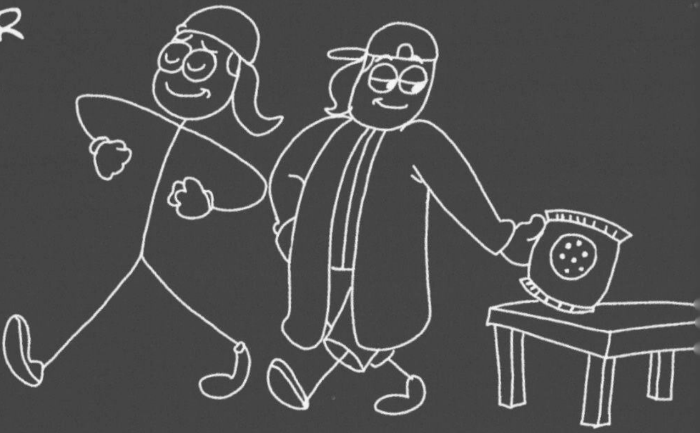

Figure B

Leave the bag on the table to go quickly jerk off

Figure C

Monster that eats cookies takes bag

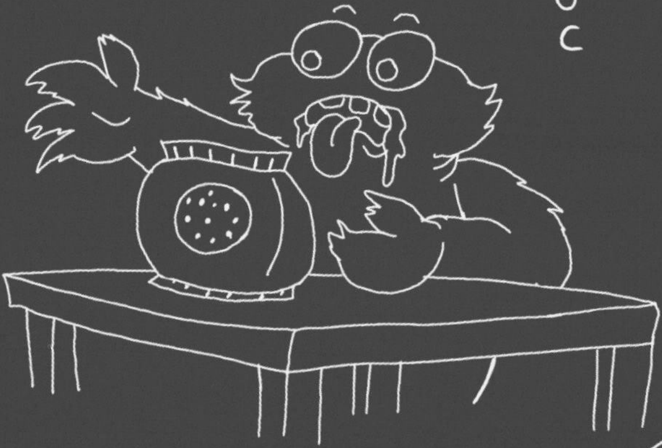

Figure D

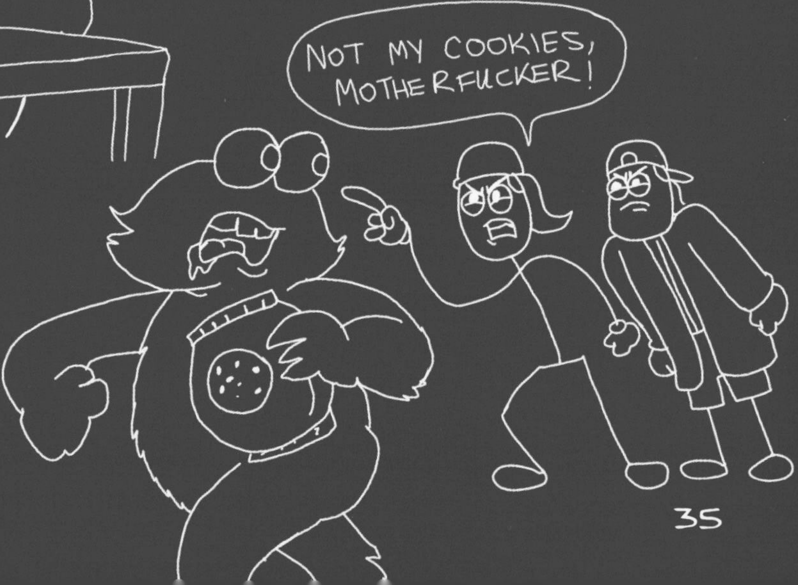
NOT MY COOKIES, MOTHERFUCKER!

OPERATION: DESTROY THE MONSTER THAT EATS COOKIES (CONT'D)

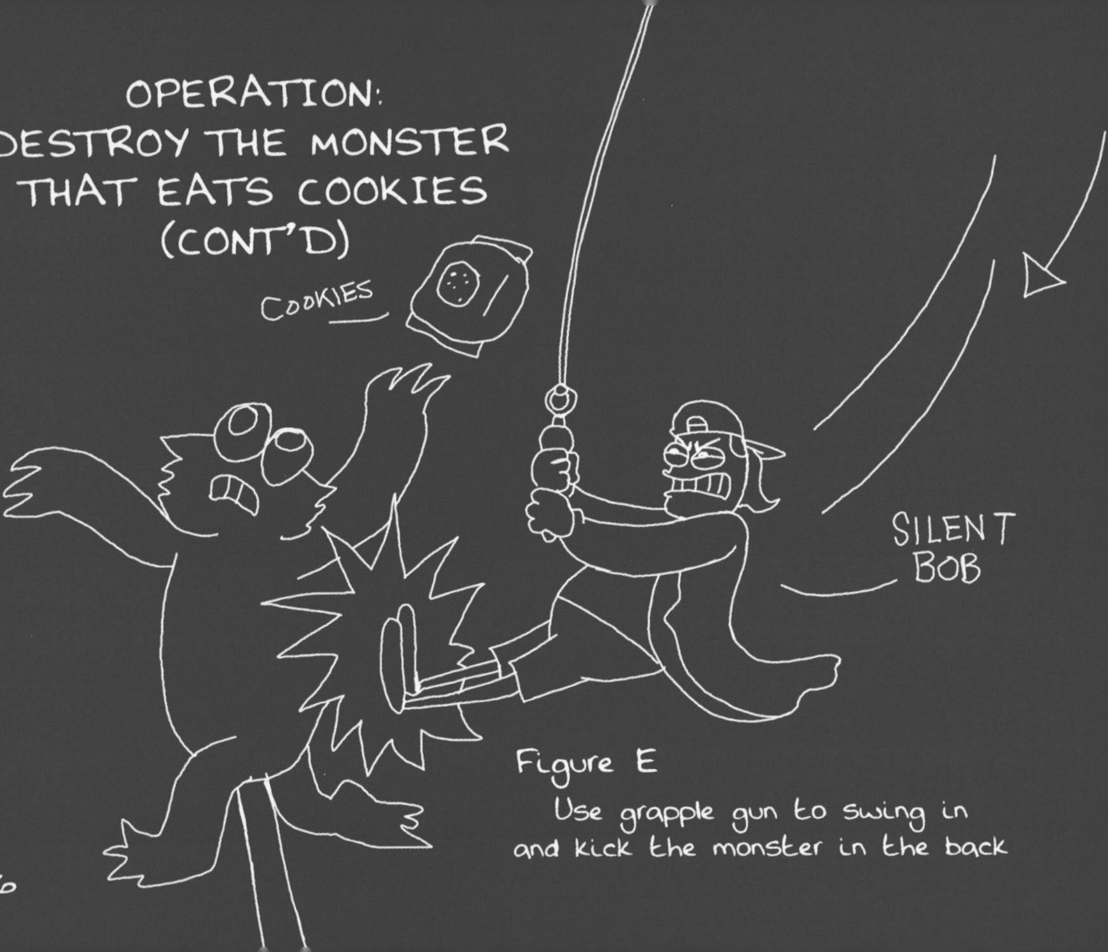
COOKIES
SILENT BOB

Figure E

Use grapple gun to swing in and kick the monster in the back

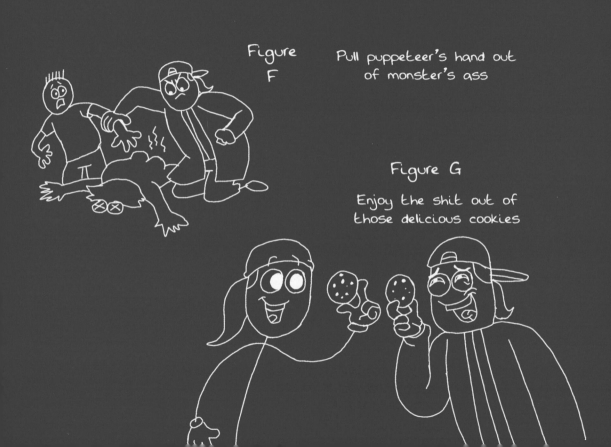

Figure
F

Pull puppeteer's hand out
of monster's ass

Figure G

Enjoy the shit out of
those delicious cookies

OPERATION: FIND THE CLITORIS

Figure A Put clit-finding boots on

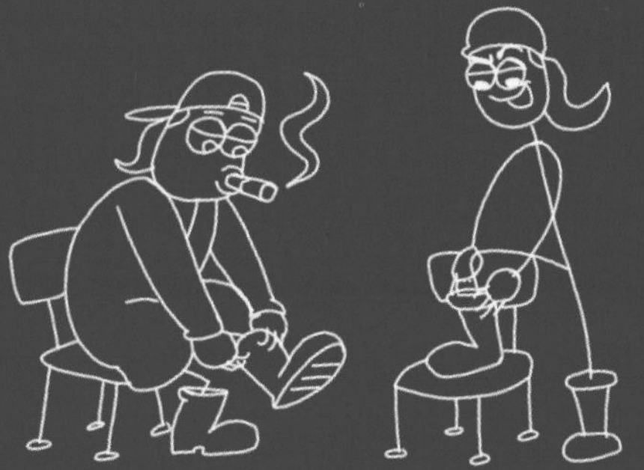

Figure B Go to the room at the end of INDIANA JONES

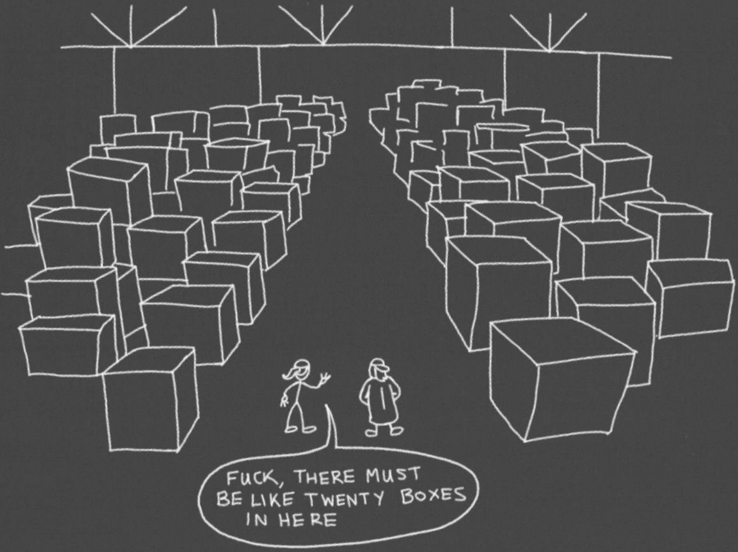
FUCK, THERE MUST BE LIKE TWENTY BOXES IN HERE

Figure C

Find an Ark and a bunch of other shit

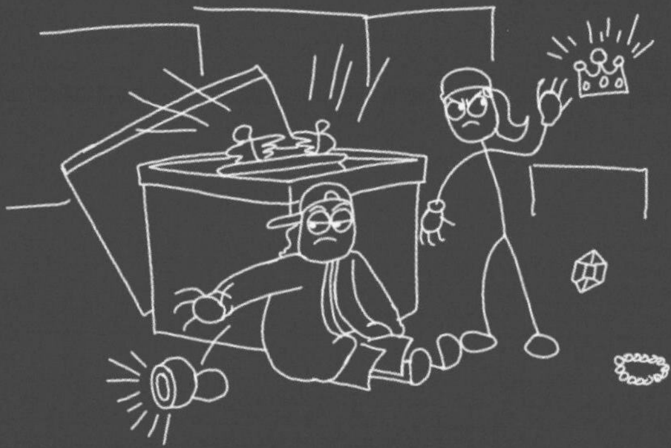

Figure D

At long last, find what must be the clitoris

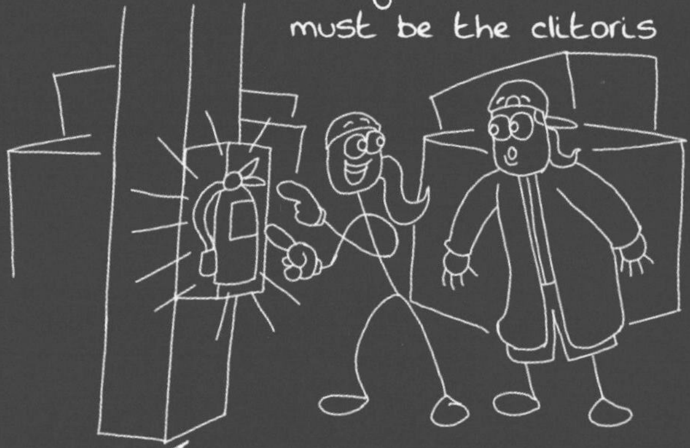

Figure E

Stroll outta there like a bunch of clit-having champs

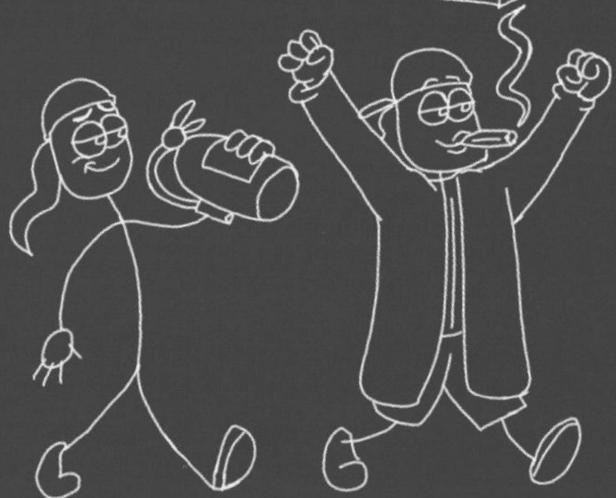

OPERATION: DESTROY THE CLIT
(IN A GOOD WAY)

Figure A

Show your lady that you truly
are a Clit Commander

Figure B

WHENEVER SHE SEES HER
CLIT, SHE'LL SEE THIS FUCKING FACE

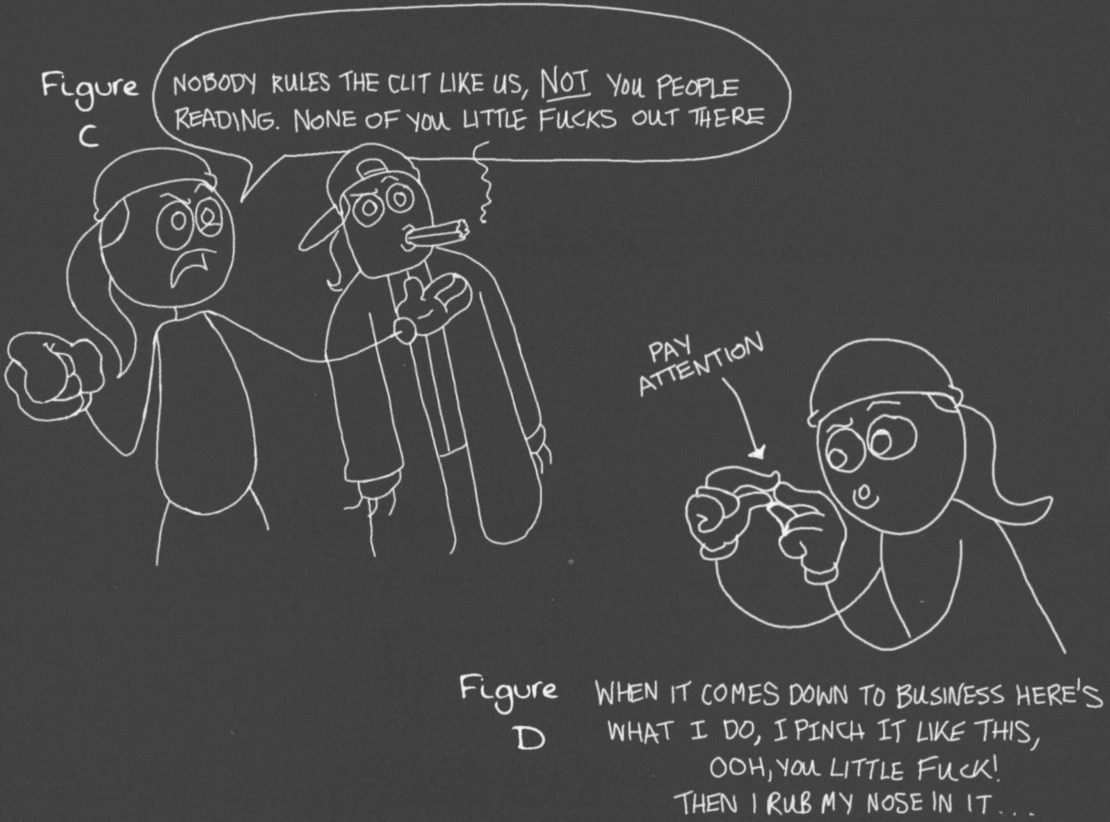
Figure C
NOBODY RULES THE CLIT LIKE US, NOT YOU PEOPLE READING. NONE OF YOU LITTLE FUCKS OUT THERE
PAY ATTENTION
Figure D
WHEN IT COMES DOWN TO BUSINESS HERE'S WHAT I DO, I PINCH IT LIKE THIS, OOH, YOU LITTLE FUCK! THEN I RUB MY NOSE IN IT...

OPERATION: DESTROY THE DINOSAURS

Figure
A

Find some old
bugs

Figure
B

Extract dinosaur
DNA from bloodsucker

42

Figure
C

Decant, centrifuge, and splice that shit and witness the miracle of life

Figure
D

Kick the shit out of it

43

OPERATION: DESTROY TRAFFIC

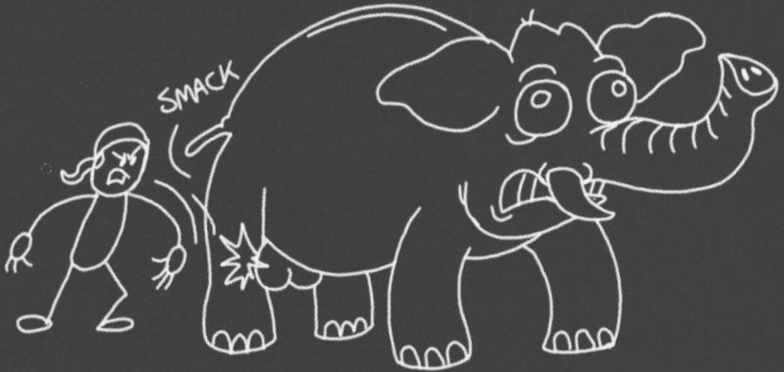
SMACK

Figure A

Locate an elephant and smack it in the nuts

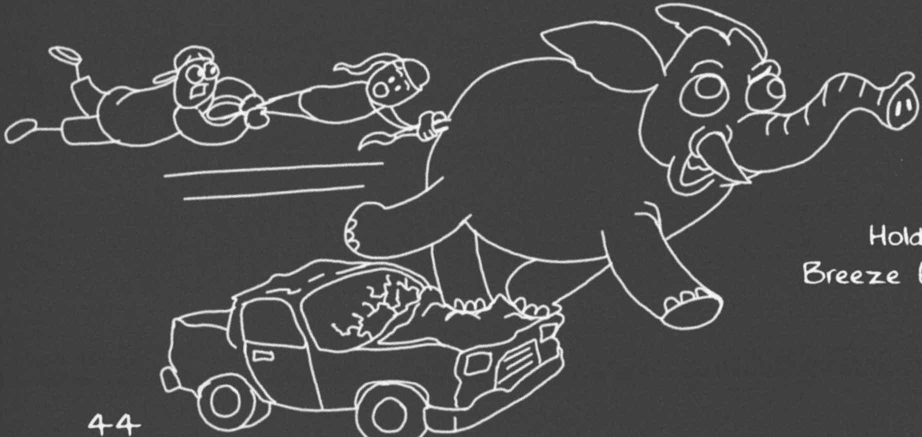

Figure B

Hold the fuck on! Breeze through traffic!

Figure C
Get to work on time

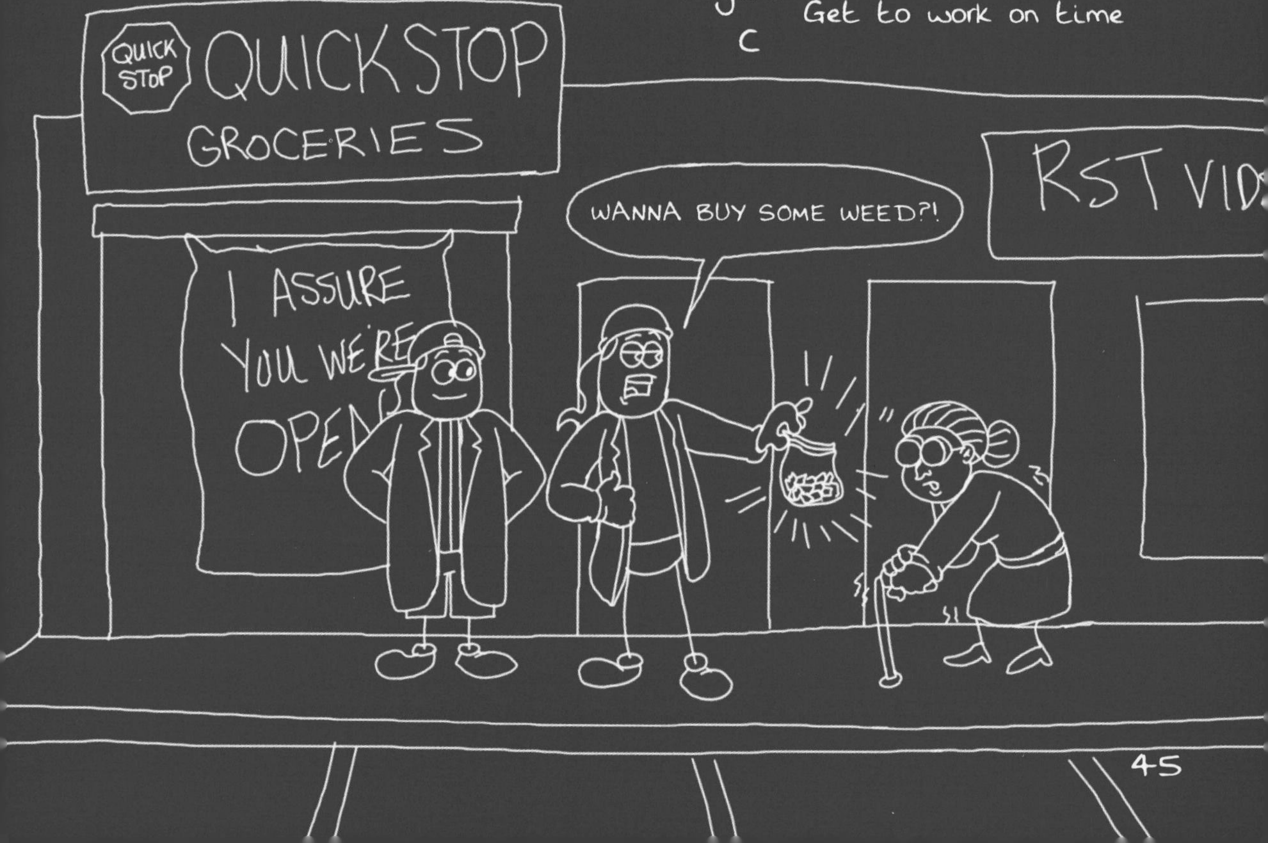

OPERATION: DESTROY HITLER

WHOAAA!
40's
60's
70's
80's
90's
2000's

Figure A

Go back in time

Figure B

Find baby Hitler

GAA
GAA
GOO
GOO

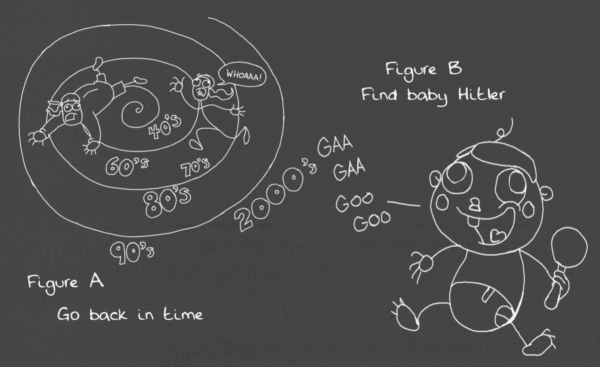

Figure C Uppercut that baby like crazy

SMACK!

WHACK!

Figure D
Boot that baby to the stars

KICK!

Figure E
Fuck you, baby Hitler!

47

OPERATION:
DESTROY COMIC CON

Figure A

Try to get into hall H
for comic book movie panel

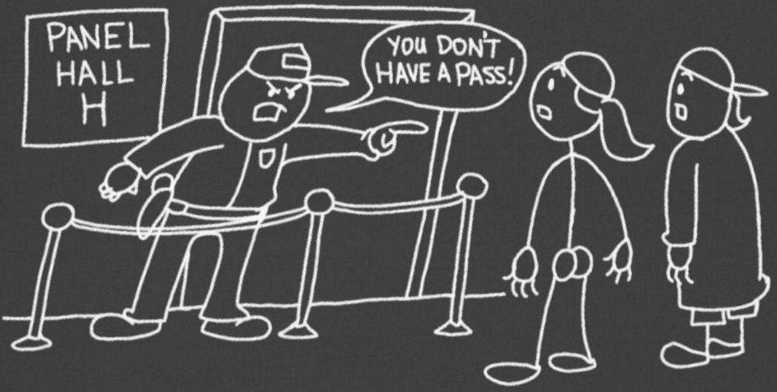
PANEL HALL H
YOU DON'T HAVE A PASS!

Figure B

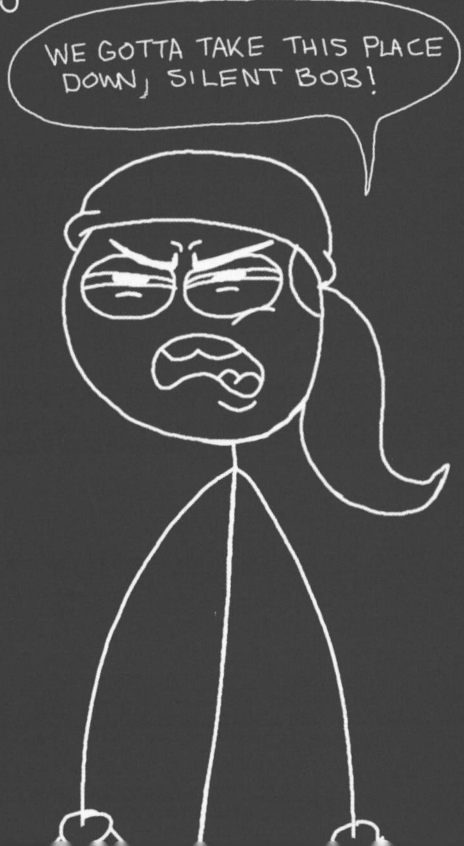
WE GOTTA TAKE THIS PLACE DOWN, SILENT BOB!

Figure C

Tell Trekkies and Whovians that the Wookies are talking shit

Figure D

Tell the Bikini Leias and fat Batmans that the Vulcans called them re-TARDIS

49

OPERATION: DESTROY COMIC CON (CONT'D)

Figure E

CIVIL WAR ENSUES!

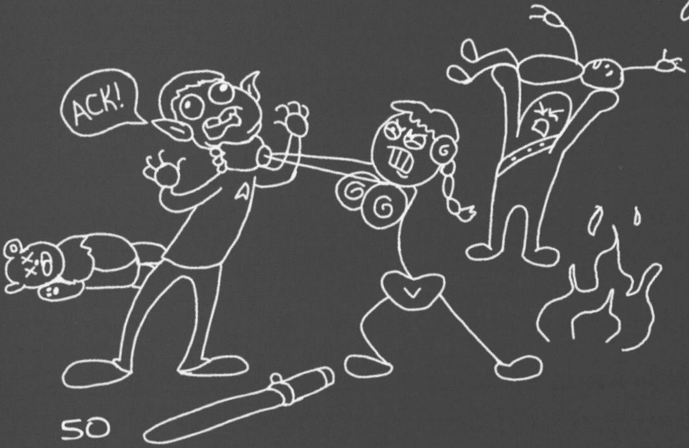
ACK!

Figure F

Crowd thins itself

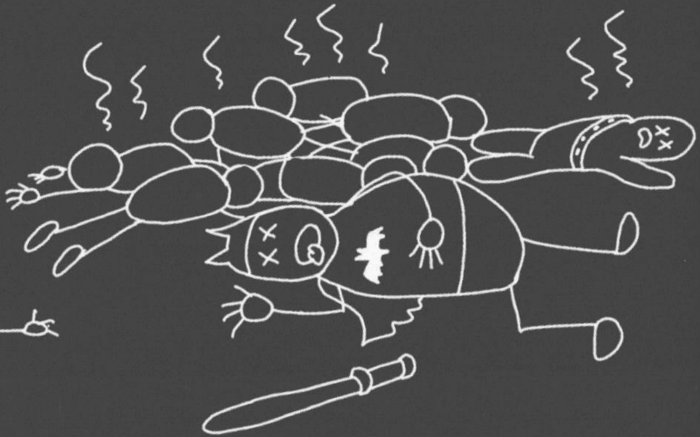

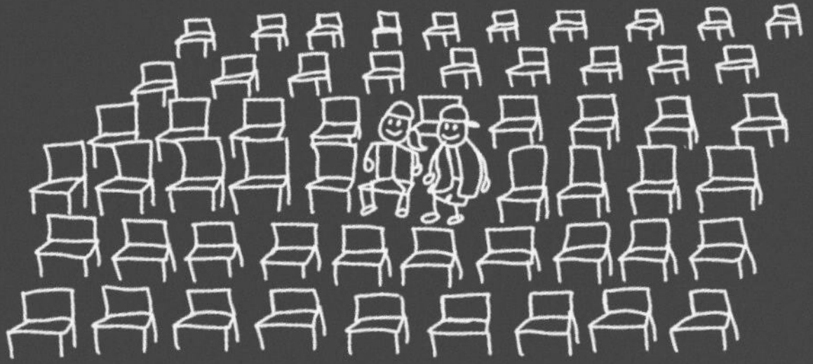

Figure G

Lots of elbow room in Hall H now

Figure H

Pitch Robert Downey, Jr. a script for IRON MAN 42

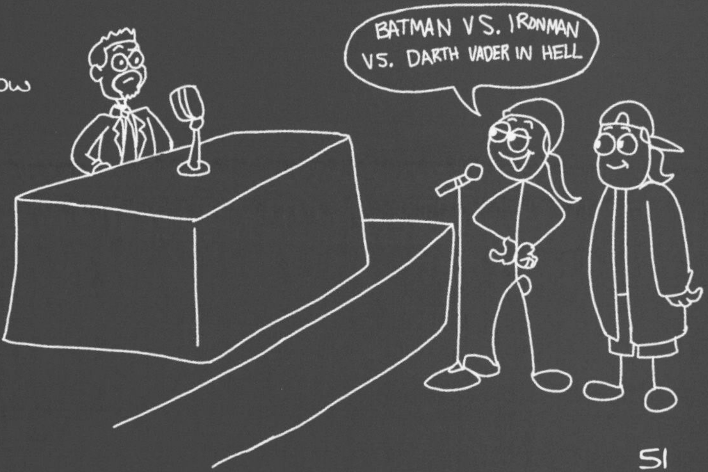
BATMAN VS. IRONMAN VS. DARTH VADER IN HELL

OPERATION: DESTROY DATING BY LEARNING TO SUCK ONE'S OWN DICK

Figure A Light some candles

Figure B Drizzle rose petals over the bed

Figure C Put on some mood music

Figure
D

Run across the room naked
and jump as high as possible, trying
to get one's cock in one's mouth

Figure
E

Smash into the headboard,
breaking own neck. Sucking one's
own dick is just a dream, a faded,
beautiful dream....

OPERATION: DESTROY BIKERS THAT RIDE ON THE SIDEWALK

Figure A

Get nearly hit by some biking calamity on a 10-speed

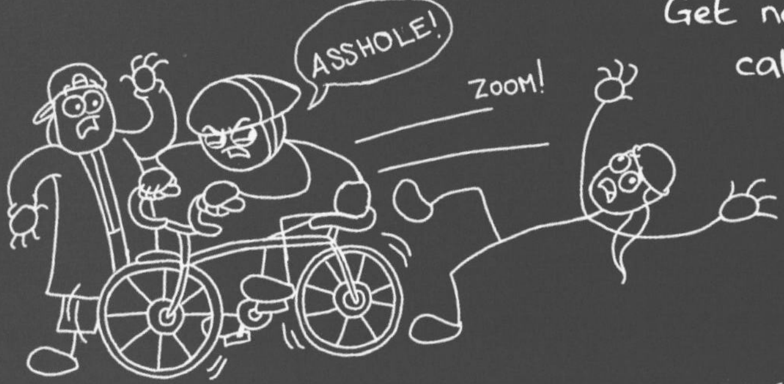
ASSHOLE!
ZOOM!

Figure B

Yell

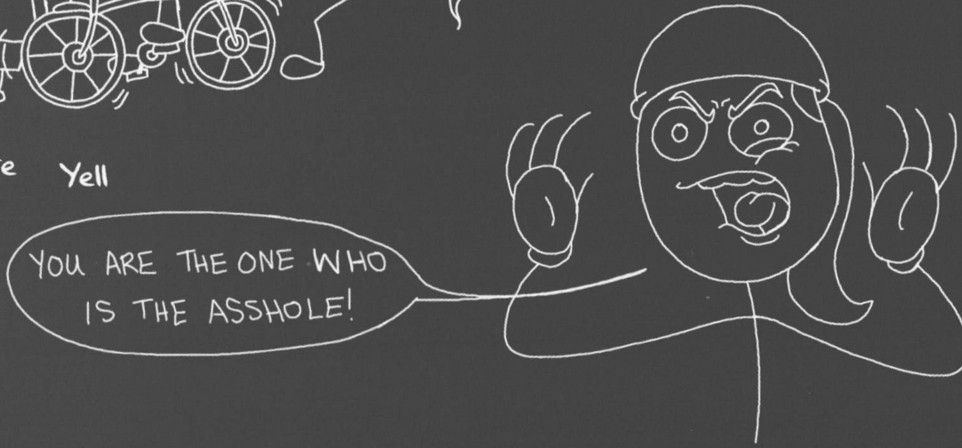
YOU ARE THE ONE WHO IS THE ASSHOLE!

Figure C

Set up spring board

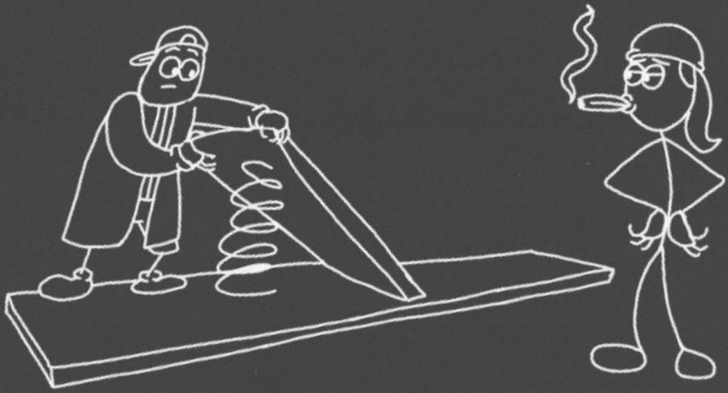

Figure D

Wait for Johnny two-wheels

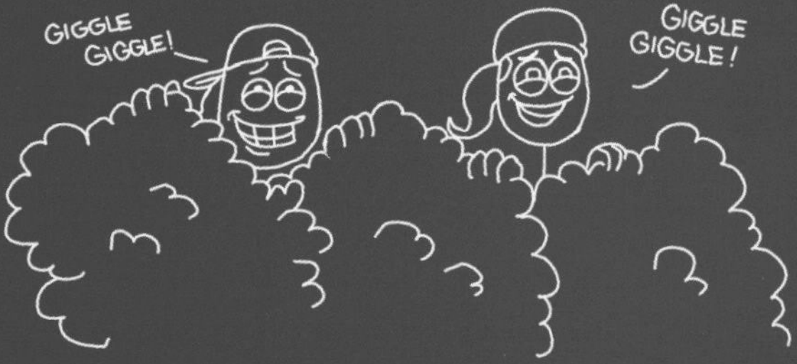
GIGGLE GIGGLE!
GIGGLE GIGGLE!

Figure E

Launch that fuck into the trash

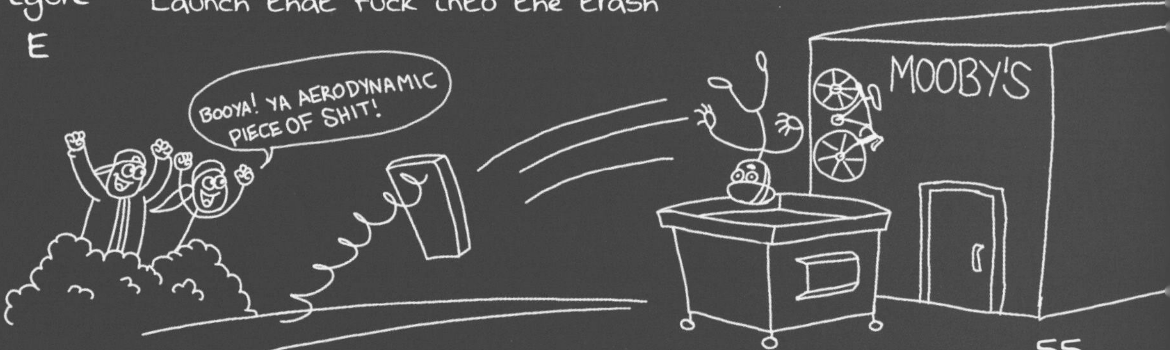
BOOYA! YA AERODYNAMIC PIECE OF SHIT!
MOOBY'S

OPERATION: DESTROY ERECTILE DYSFUNCTION

Figure B
Get some duct tape and a pack of hotdogs

Figure A
Lose boner

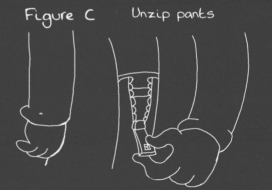

Figure C   Unzip pants

Figure D

Tape bathroom medicine cabinet open with hotdog and pants

Figure E

Take erectile dysfunction pills from the medicine cabinet - Enjoy your awesome boner!

OPERATION: DESTROY FAT HATIN' AIRLINES

Figure A

Stupid airline fucks with my boy!

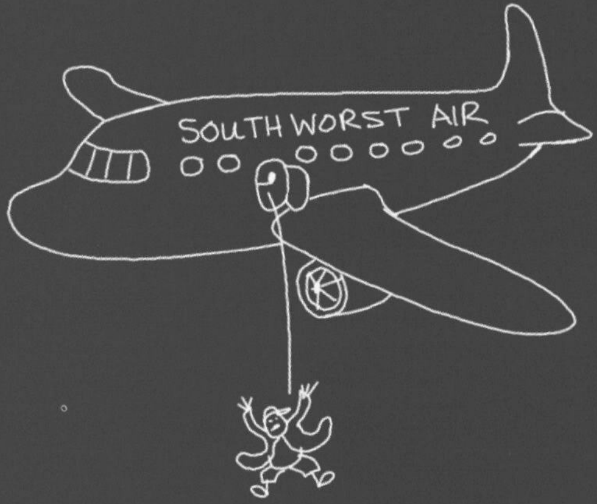
SOUTH WORST AIR

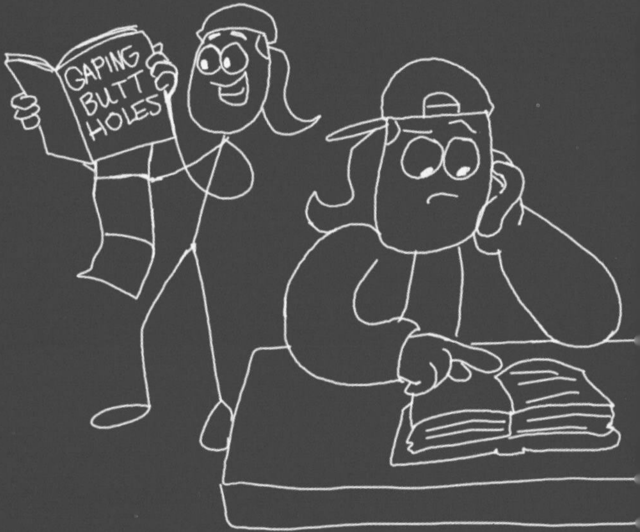
GAPING BUTT HOLES

Figure B

Jay and Bob crack the books

Figure C Build world's first teleportation device

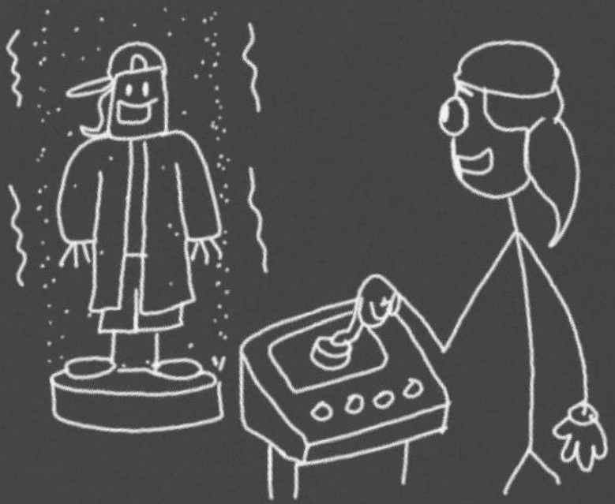

Figure D
Beat the plane to destination

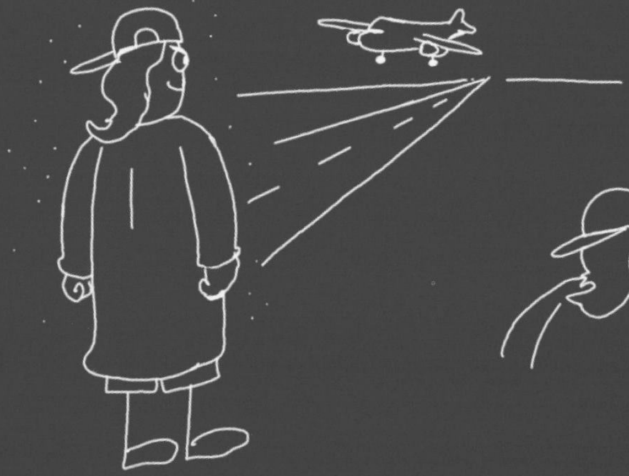

Figure E

Hurl shit at them when they open the door upon arrival

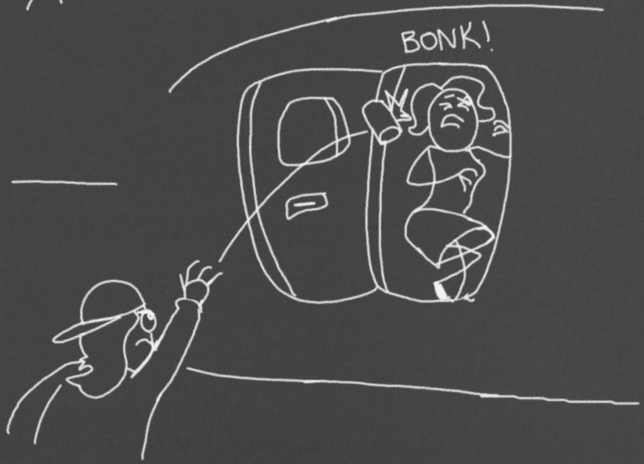
BONK!

OPERATION: DESTROY THE EYE OF SAURON

Figure A

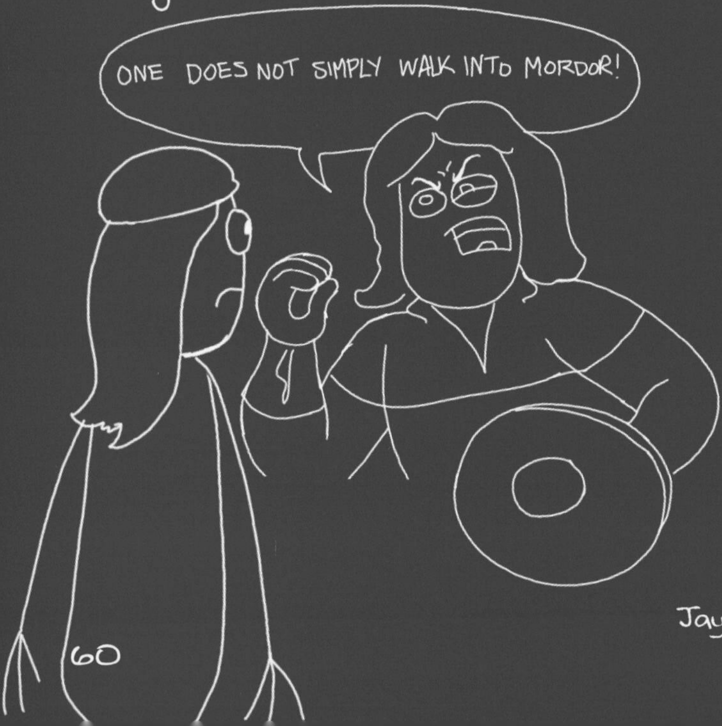
ONE DOES NOT SIMPLY WALK INTO MORDOR!

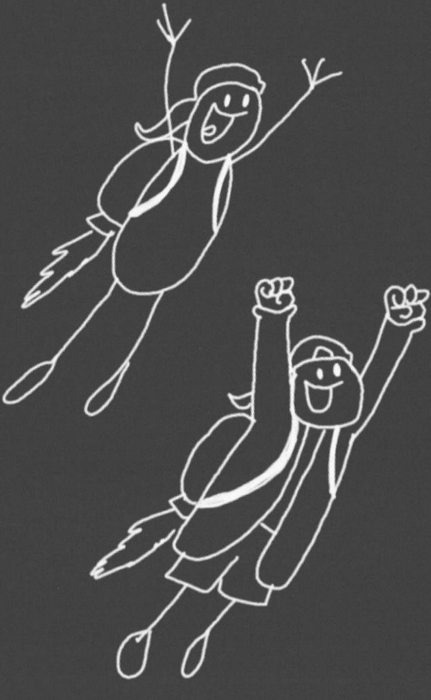

Figure B
Jay and Bob JET PACK into Mordor!

Figure C

Drop shit on Orc army from above!

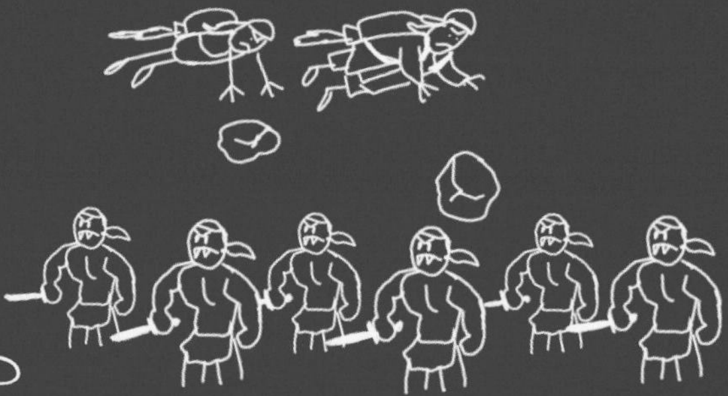

Figure D

Piss in the Eye of Sauron!

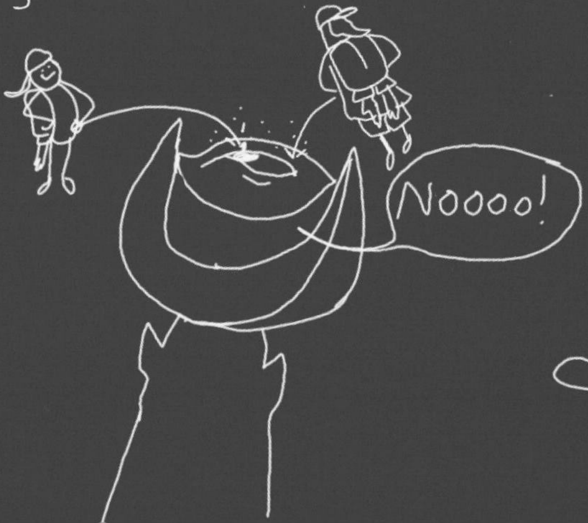
Noooo!

Figure E

Get high with an Elf Princess!!!

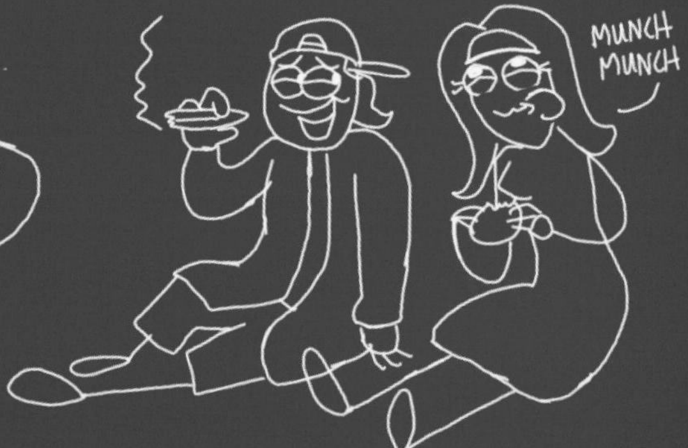
MUNCH
MUNCH

OPERATION: DESTROY SPAWN CAMPERS

Figure A

Jay and Bob put in their favorite shooter

Figure B

Go online

o CAMPAIGN
o MULTIPLAYER
o OPTIONS
CALL OF THE BATTLEFIELD
SEX-BOX

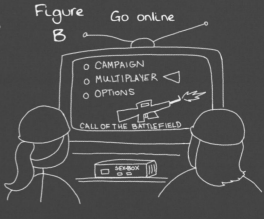

Figure C

Die and be repeatedly killed as character spawns

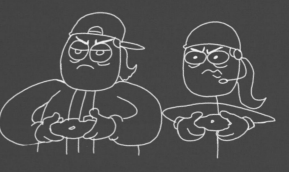

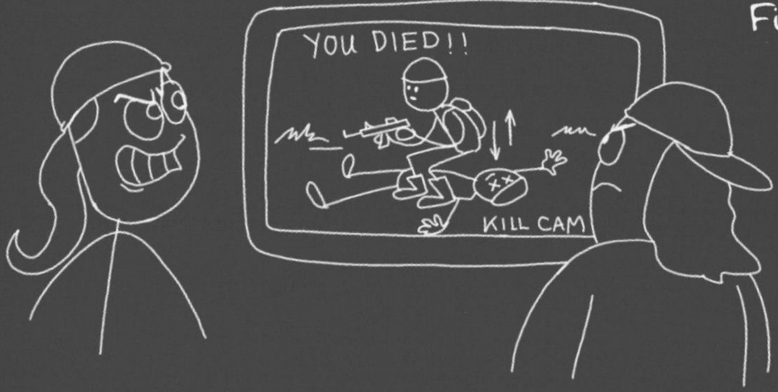
YOU DIED!!
KILL CAM

Figure D

Be teabagged on own TV screen

Figure E

Get Silent Bob to track down the gamer's whereabouts from his IP address

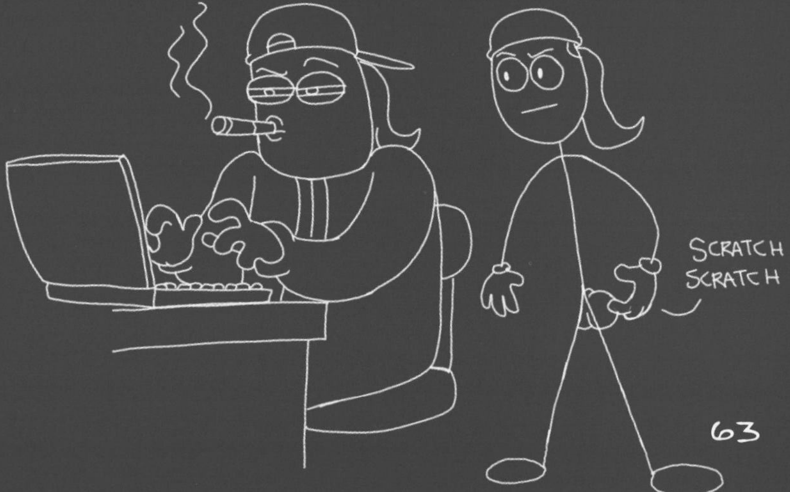
SCRATCH
SCRATCH

OPERATION: DESTROY SPAWN CAMPERS (CONT'D)

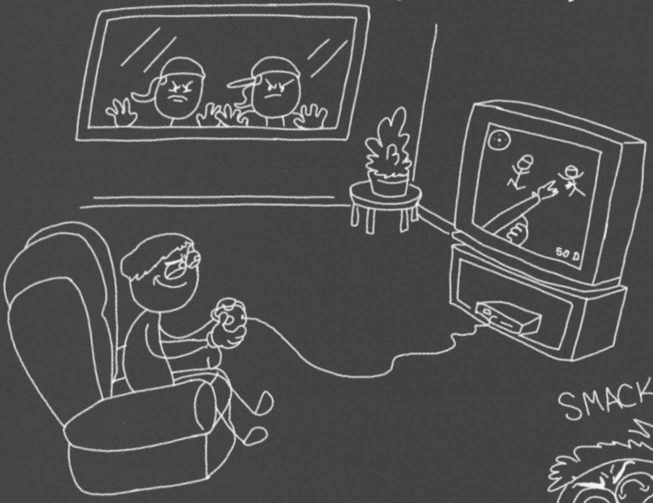

Figure F

Go to his house and see that fucker sitting in his living room

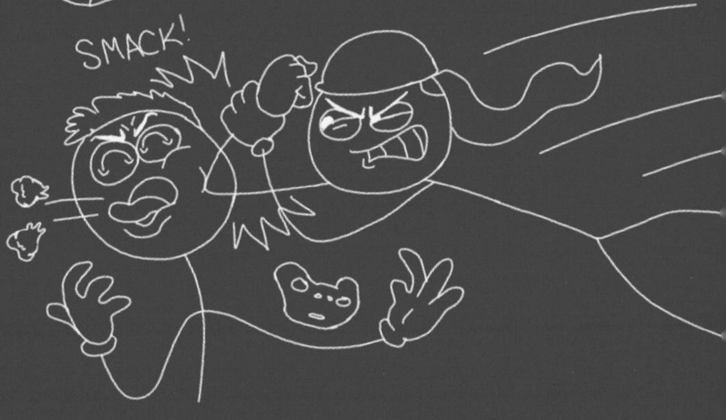
SMACK!

Figure G

Take him out with a hucklebuck

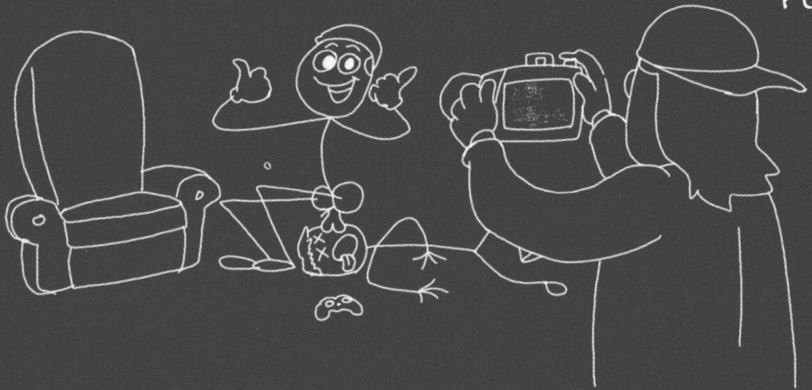

Figure H

Teabag the douche while Silent Bob takes pictures

Figure I

Leave the picture taped to his TV

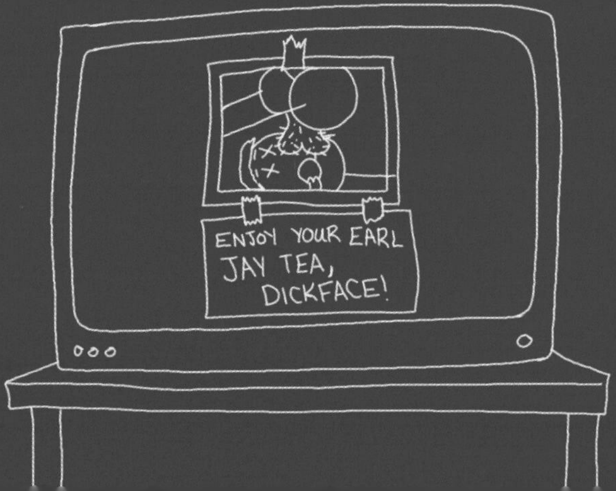
ENJOY YOUR EARL JAY TEA, DICKFACE!

OPERATION: DESTROY THAT GUY THAT KEEPS SHITTING IN JAY'S PANTS

Figure A
Wake up and see someone shit in Jay's pants again

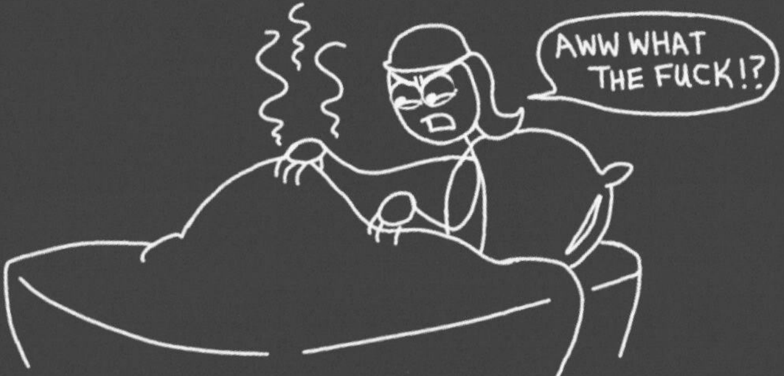
AWW WHAT THE FUCK!?

Figure B
Inform Silent Bob

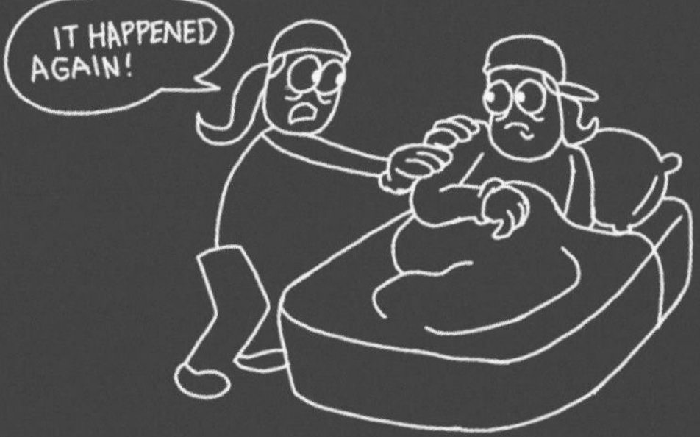
IT HAPPENED AGAIN!

Figure C
Interrogate the neighbors

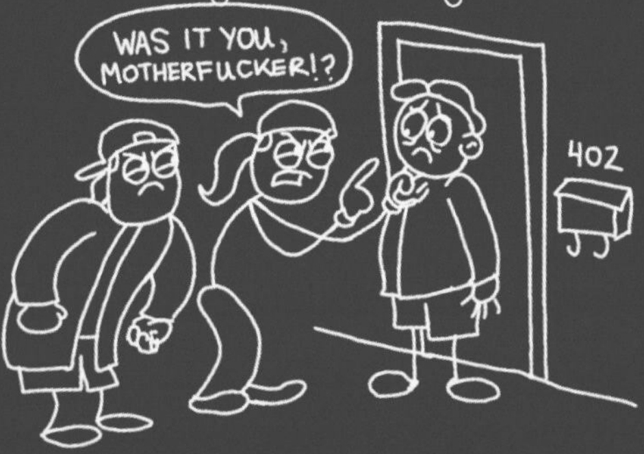
WAS IT YOU, MOTHERFUCKER!?
402

Figure D
Become very tired after a day of searching

Figure E
Have a few chocolates before bed

MUNCH MUNCH

CHOCOLATE LAXATIVES

ZZZZz

Figure F
Put the case on unsolved –
Go to sleep/repeat

67

OPERATION:
DESTROY USELESS DVD LIBRARY

BLU-RAYS

BRAND NEW!!
$ EXPENSIVE!! $

DVD

DOG SHIT

Figure
A

Blu-rays come out,
making DVDs useless

Figure B

Dump over shelf
of DVDs

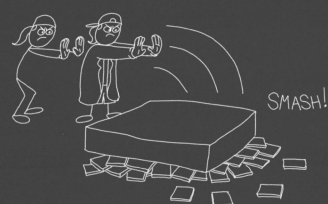

SMASH!

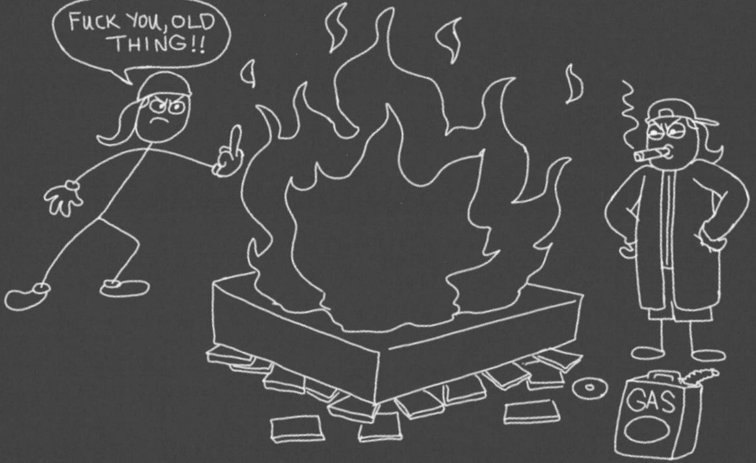
FUCK YOU, OLD THING!!
GAS

Figure C

Light DVD collection on fire

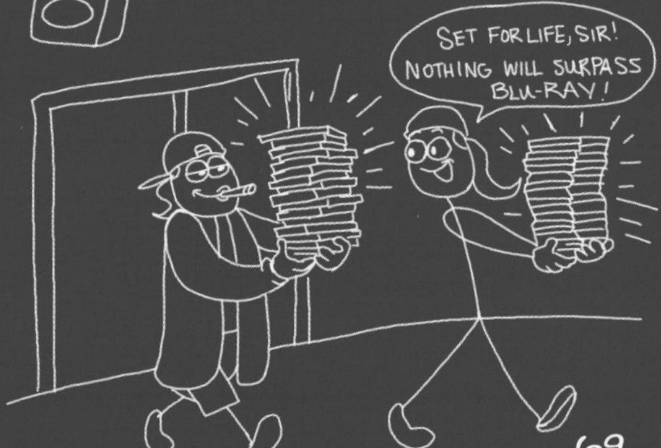
SET FOR LIFE, SIR! NOTHING WILL SURPASS BLU-RAY!

Figure D

Empty bank account purchasing movie library again on Blu-ray

OPERATION: DESTROY THE DENTIST

Figure A

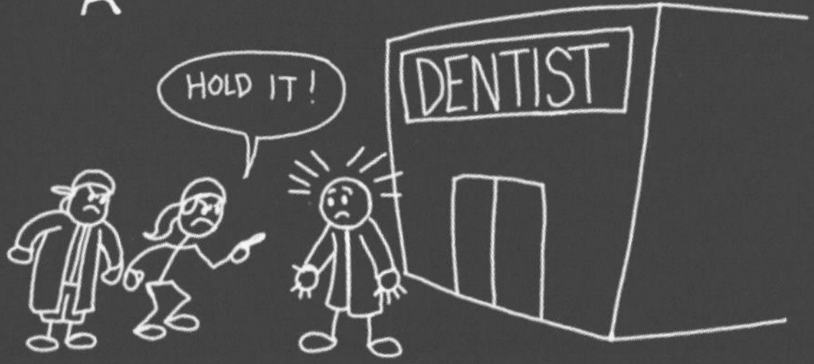
HOLD IT!
DENTIST

Find that motherfucker that fucks with teeth

Figure B

Explain that we don't need him to clean our teeth!

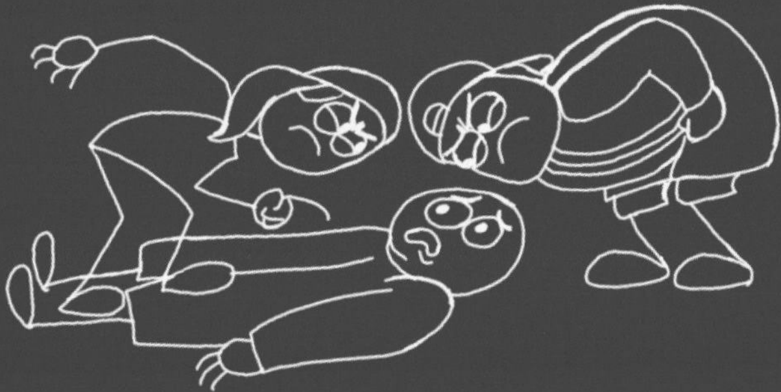

Figure
C

Smile with victory

71

OPERATION: DESTROY EROTIC FICTION

Figure A

See that the ladies are buying up these erotic 50 Shades books like HOTCAKES

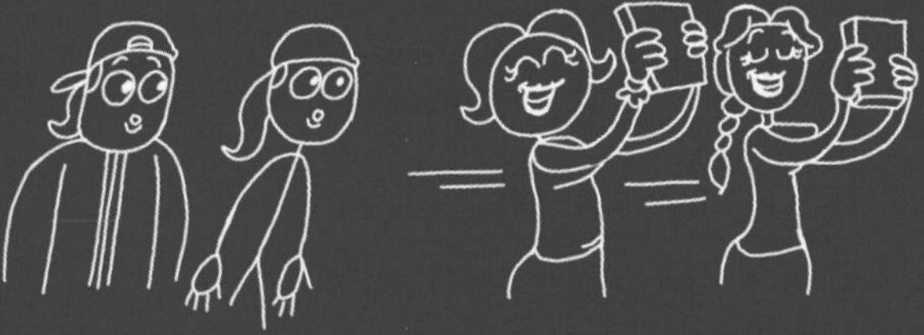

Figure B

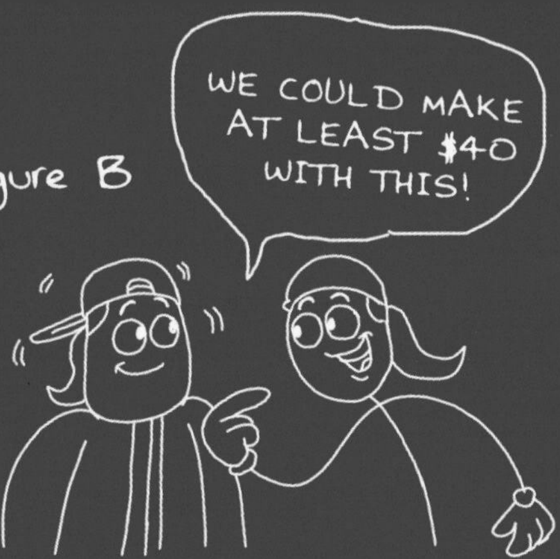
WE COULD MAKE AT LEAST $40 WITH THIS!

Figure C

Come out with 50 Shades of JAY

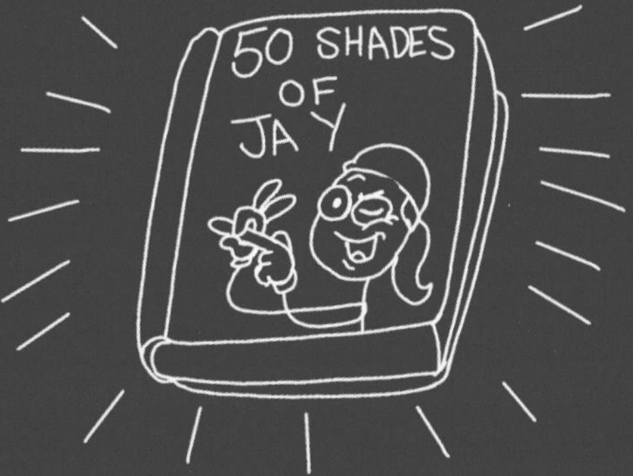
50 SHADES OF JAY

Figure D

Watch it fail when everyone realizes the book is just 100 pages of Jay's bung hole

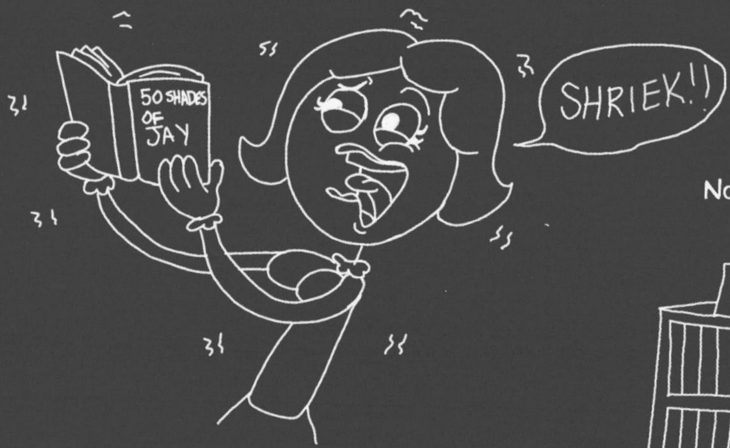
50 SHADES OF JAY
SHRIEK!!

Figure E

No one buys erotic fiction ever again

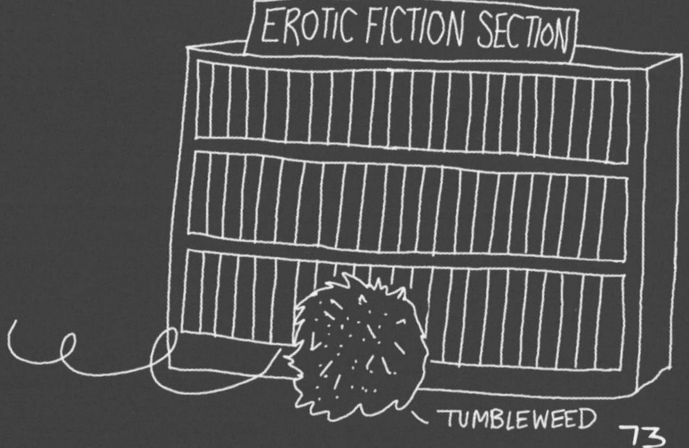
EROTIC FICTION SECTION
TUMBLEWEED

OPERATION: DESTROY CRIMINALS

Figure A

Jay and Bob establish a secret base

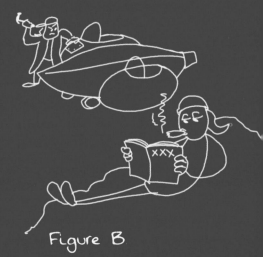

Figure B

Build a sweet-ass, specially designed motherfucker of a car with gadgets and doohickeys that can be used in a two-man war on crime

Figure C Design costumes and a shtick that'll scare the fuck out of the criminal element!

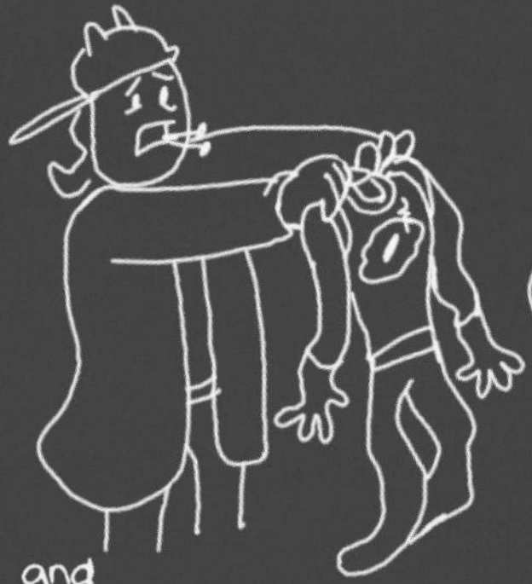

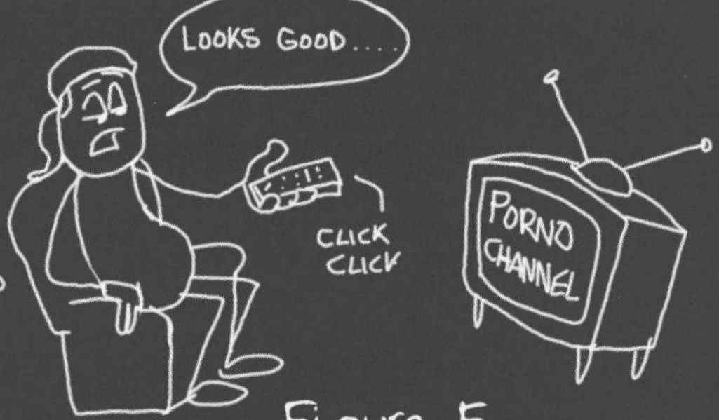
LOOKS GOOD....
CLICK CLICK
PORNO CHANNEL

Figure D
Stand on rooftop and wait for supercrime

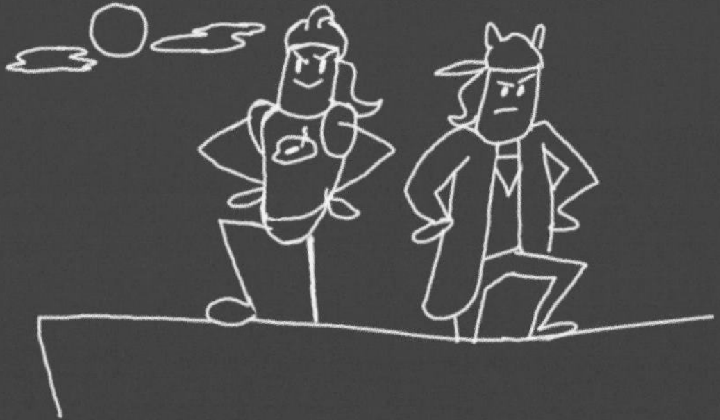

Figure E
Get bored and CREATE supervillains instead!

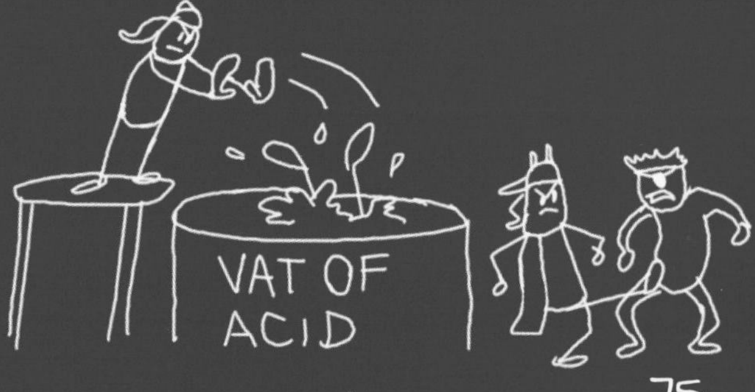
VAT OF ACID

OPERATION: DESTROY THAT DAMN DIRTY HURRICANE

Figure B

Find that dirty hurricane

Figure A

Intimidate a weatherman to tell of the hurricane's whereabouts

Figure C

Run in the opposite direction of the dickheaded weather manifestation

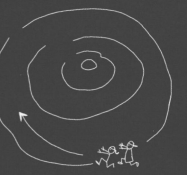

Figure D

Run right up its anus, killing it

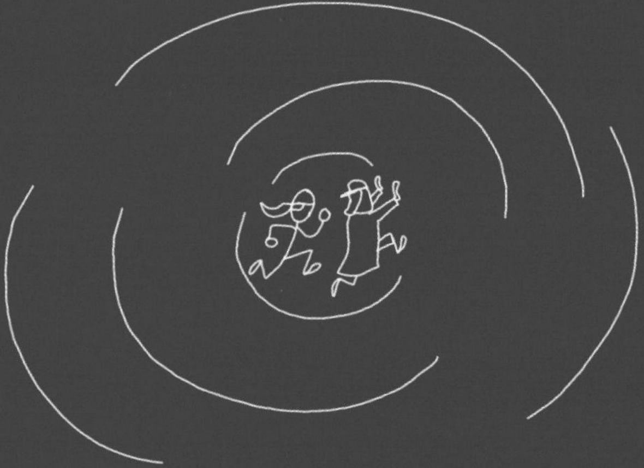

Figure E

Give lungs a break from all that running with a victory doob

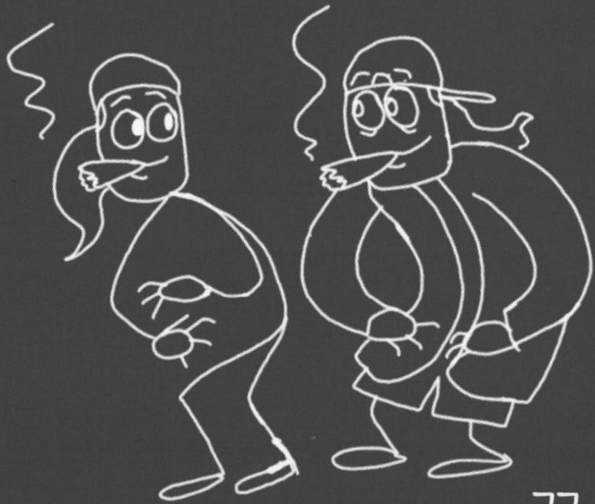

OPERATION: DESTROY THE BAN ON GAY MARRIAGE

Figure A

Jay and Bob dress up as undercover Congressmen

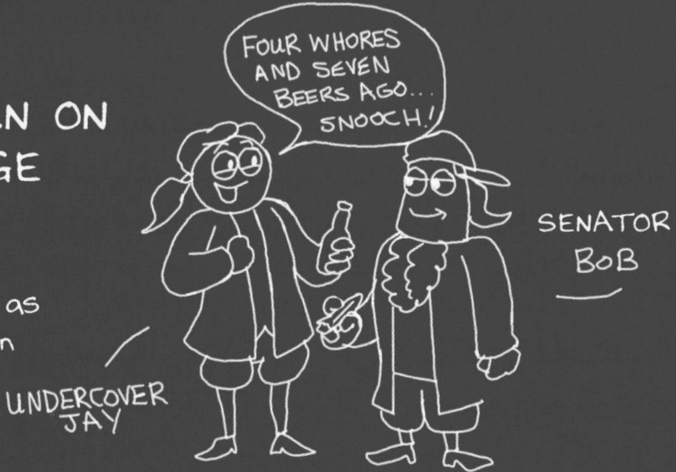
FOUR WHORES AND SEVEN BEERS AGO... SNOOCH!
SENATOR BOB
UNDERCOVER JAY

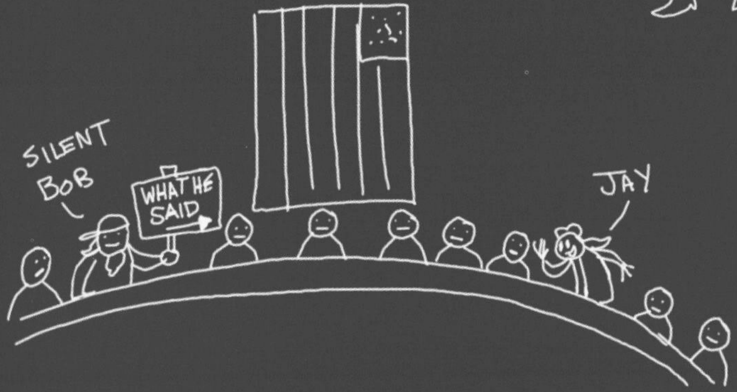
SILENT BOB
WHAT HE SAID
JAY

Figure B

Whisper and push Gay Love on the rest of the House

Figure C

Fix all of the paperwork so Nay turns to Gay and the computer pop ups to Gay Love

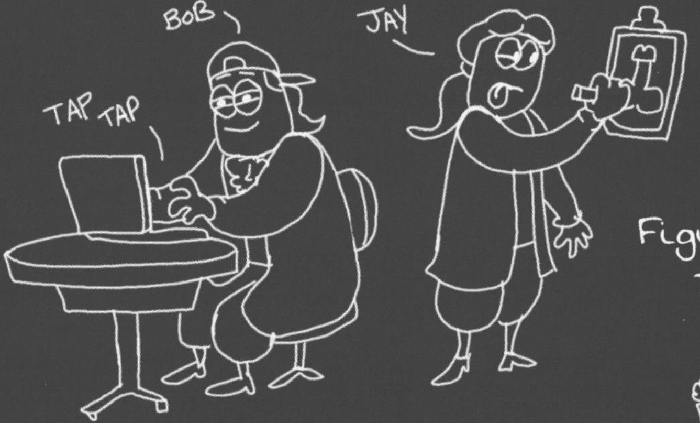
BOB
JAY
TAP TAP

Figure D

Jay and Bob get married in the house of Congress.

The congressmen make out wildly

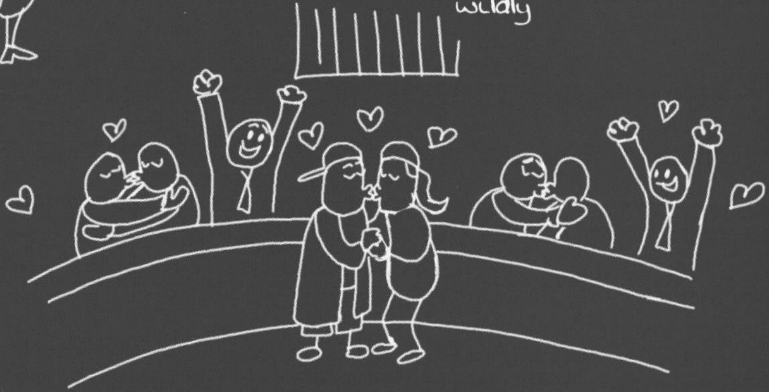

OPERATION: DESTROY PEOPLE ON THE INTERNET THAT COMPARE EVERYONE'S ACTIONS TO HITLER'S

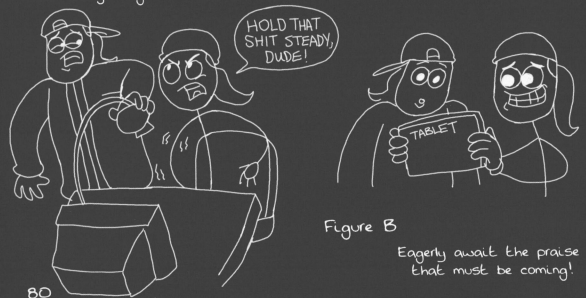

Figure A

Post a closeup video of Jay and Bob jerking off on the internet

HOLD THAT SHIT STEADY, DUDE!

TABLET

Figure B

Eagerly await the praise that must be coming!

Figure C Watch some jerkoff write that said video is worse than anything Hitler did

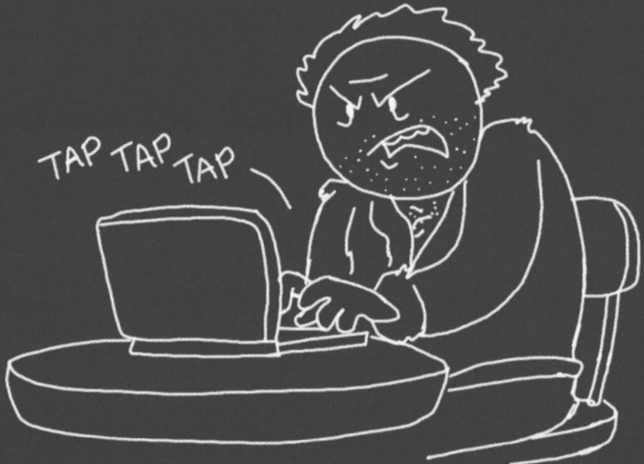
TAP TAP TAP

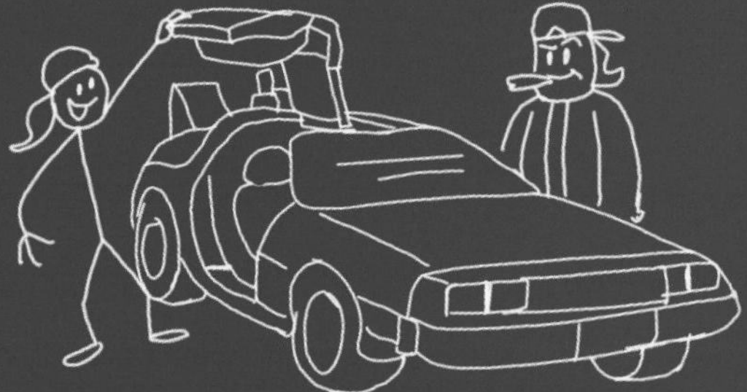

Figure D

Go back in time and take out Hitler so people can no longer bash awesome jerkoff videos

OPERATION:
DESTROY WAITING IN LINE

Figure B

Take an ordinary house cat and a
burlap sack

BOB JAY

Figure A

Get in massive lineup

SHAKE
SHAKE

Figure C

Shake the cat like
crazy

Figure D

Let the cat out of the bag

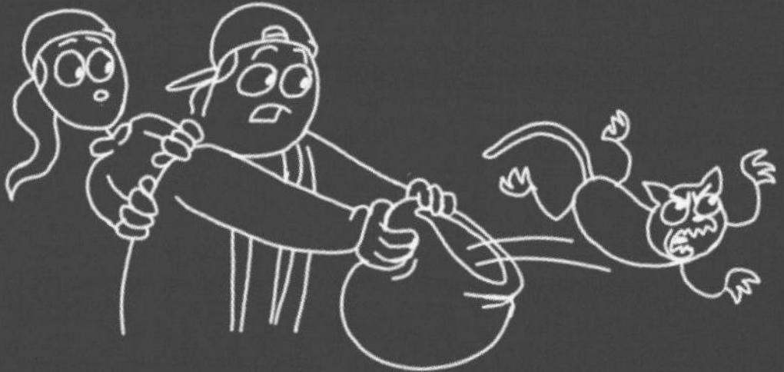

Figure E

The cat attacks all of the people

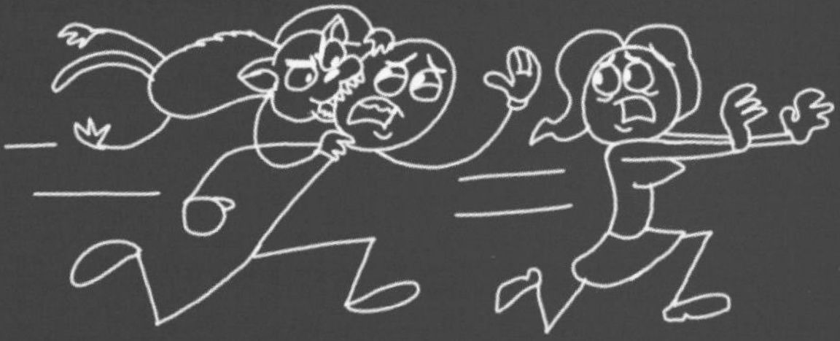

Figure F

Move to the front of the line

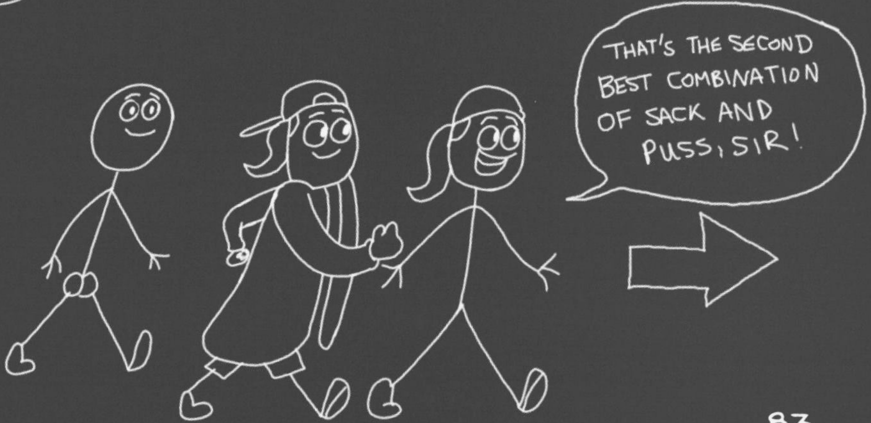
THAT'S THE SECOND BEST COMBINATION OF SACK AND PUSS, SIR!

OPERATION: DESTROY SPAM

Figure A

Get clearly ridiculous email

WAIT A SECOND, THAT WASN'T THE QUEEN OF CHINA!?

Figure B

Silent Bob hacks the spammer's email to track that motherfucker down

#

Figure C

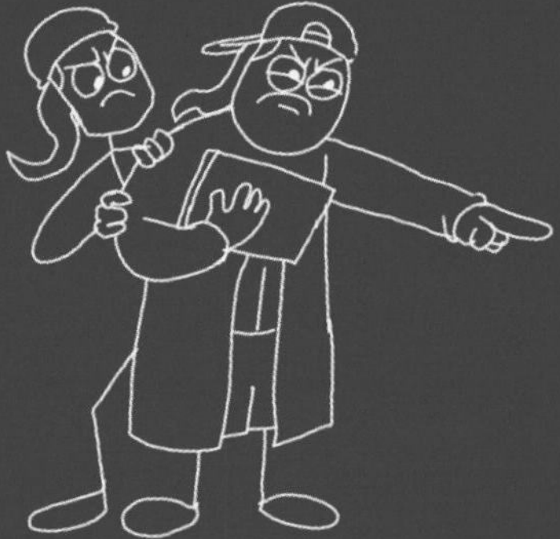

Turns out it's a nine-year-old boy from Russia

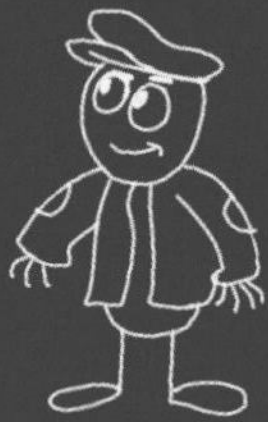

Figure D

The boy yells, "DIPLOMATIC IMMUNITY!"

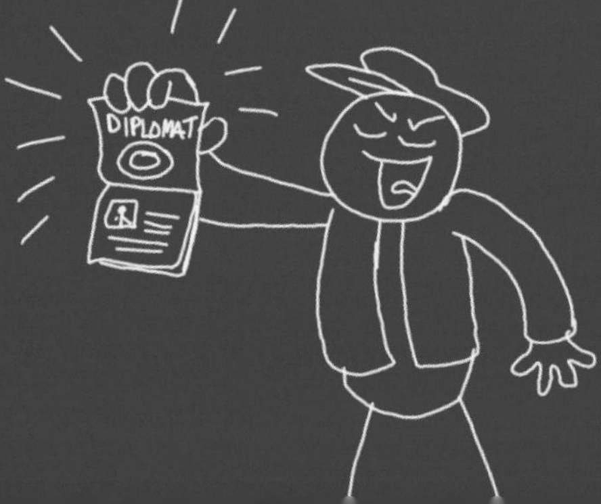
DIPLOMAT

Figure E

Jay and Bob are powerless

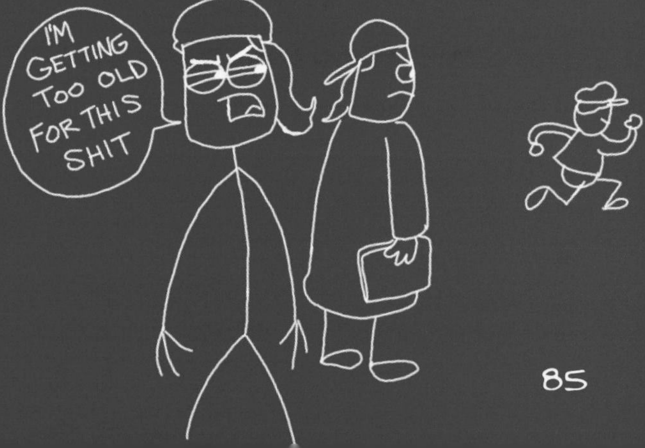
I'M GETTING TOO OLD FOR THIS SHIT

OPERATION: DESTROY THE EMPEROR IN RETURN OF THE JEDI

Figure A

In JEDI, Luke goes to strike down the Emperor and Vader blocks his shot

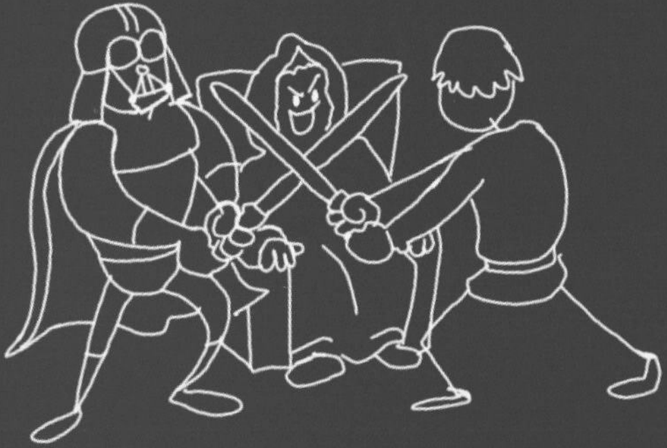

Figure B

Deduce where Luke went wrong

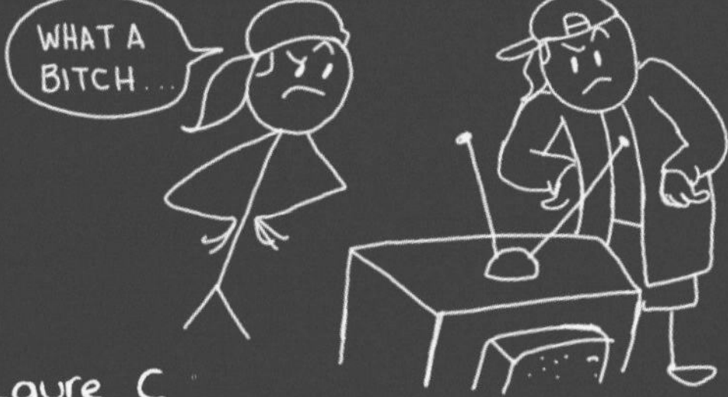
WHAT A BITCH...

Figure C

Re-create the moment in real life

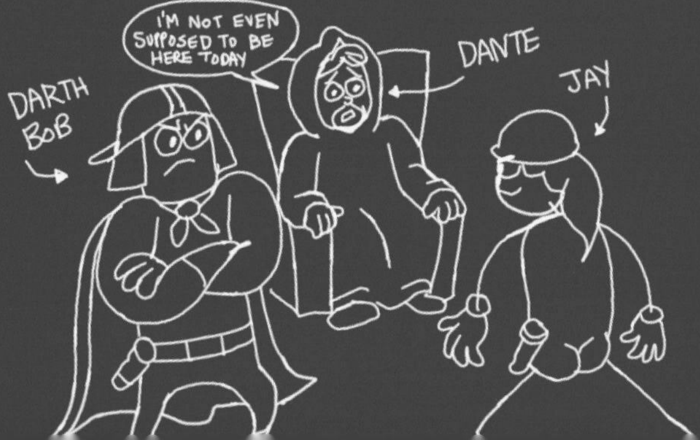
I'M NOT EVEN SUPPOSED TO BE HERE TODAY
DARTH BOB
DANTE
JAY

Figure D

Swing AROUND the chair and cut his head off from behind

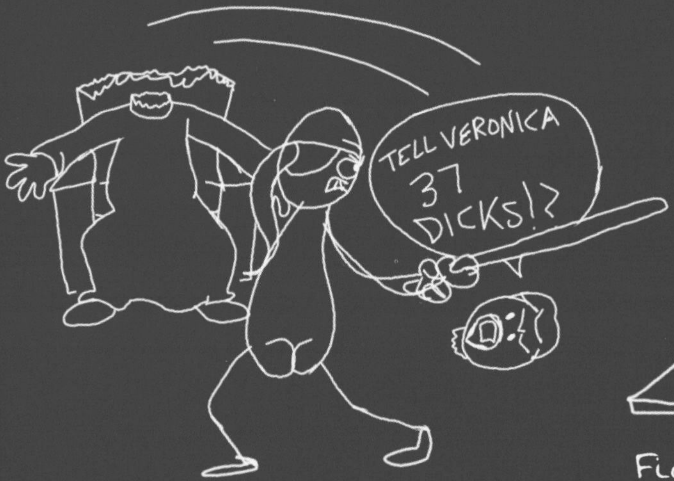
TELL VERONICA 37 DICKS!?

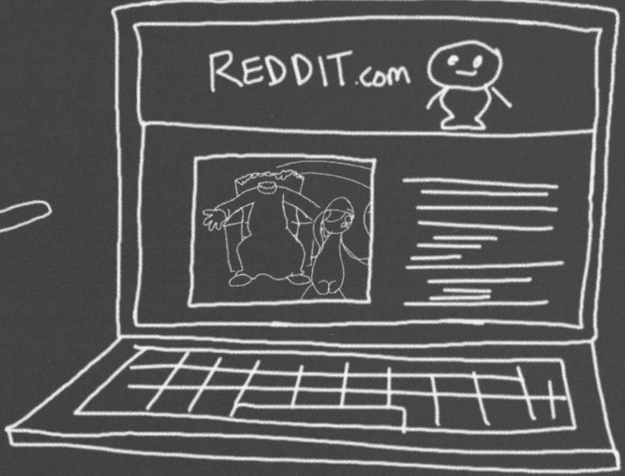
REDDIT.com

Figure E

Meme hits front page of Reddit

OPERATION: DESTROY SMELLY FARTS

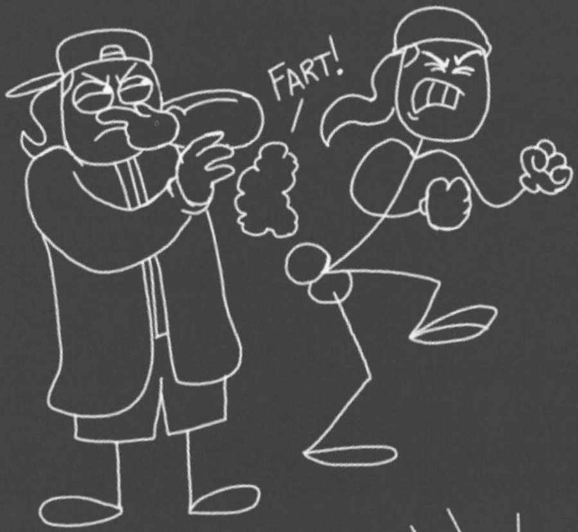
FART!

Figure A

Can't stop farting

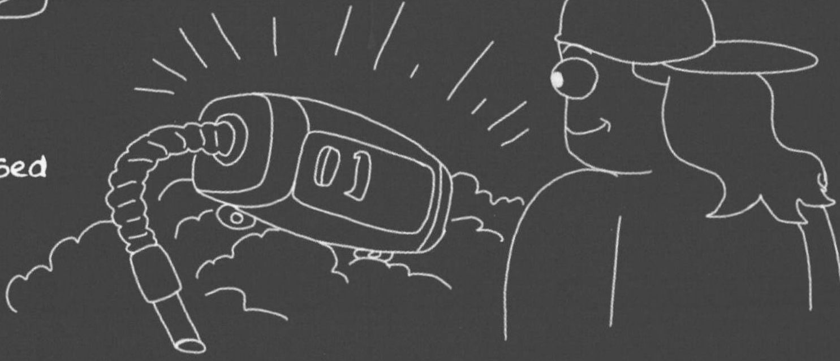
01

Figure B

Find that unused vacuum

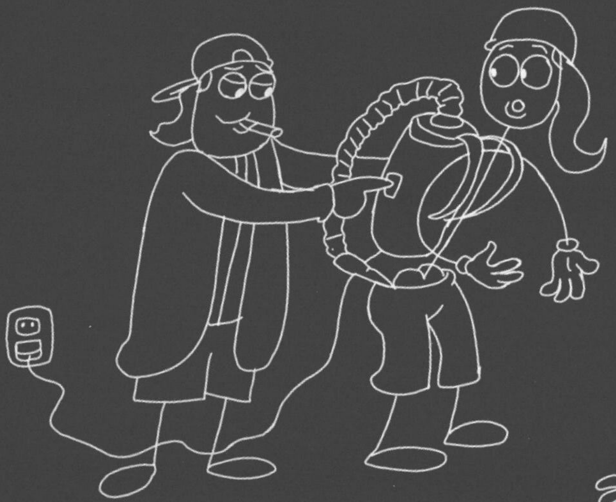

Figure C

Strap the vacuum to your back with the nozzle in your pants

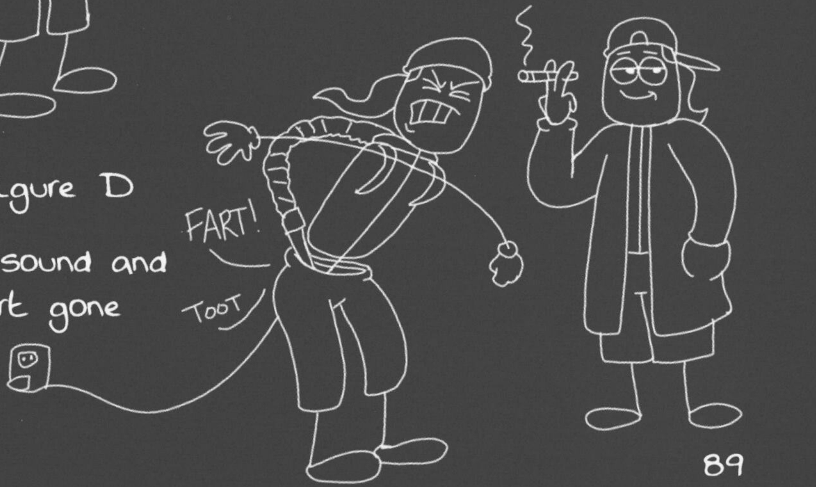
FART!
TOOT

Figure D

Turn it on - sound and smell of fart gone

OPERATION: DESTROY GOING TO THE DOCTOR'S

Figure A

Fuck needles and getting a finger up the ass ever again!

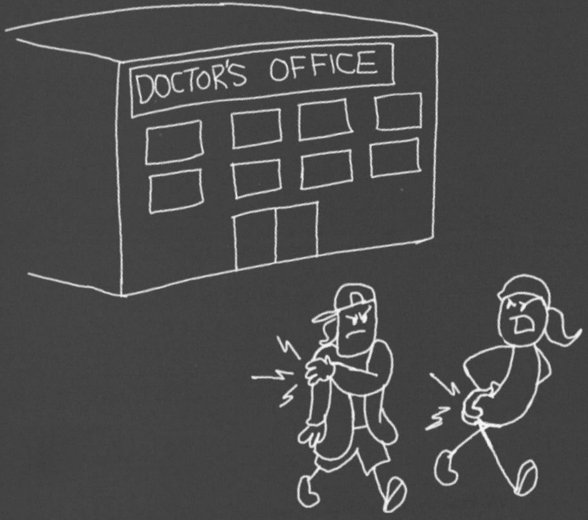
DOCTOR'S OFFICE

Figure B

Crack the books!

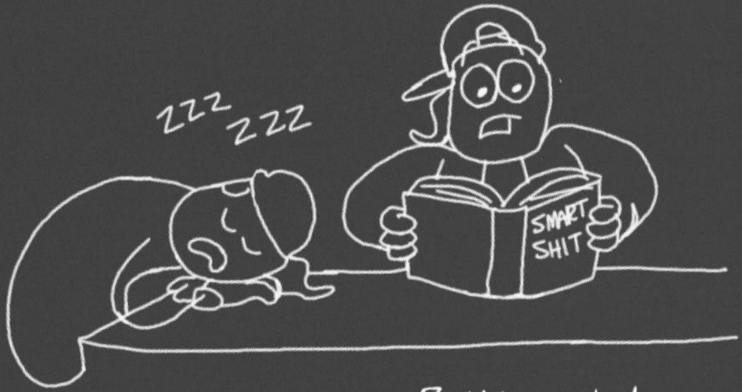
ZZZ ZZZ
SMART SHIT

Figure C

Build a robot

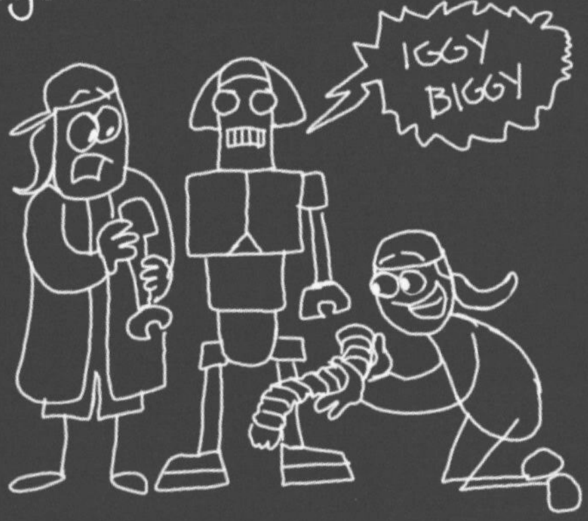
IGGY BIGGY

Figure D

Then build a Doctor Robot for him to carry around

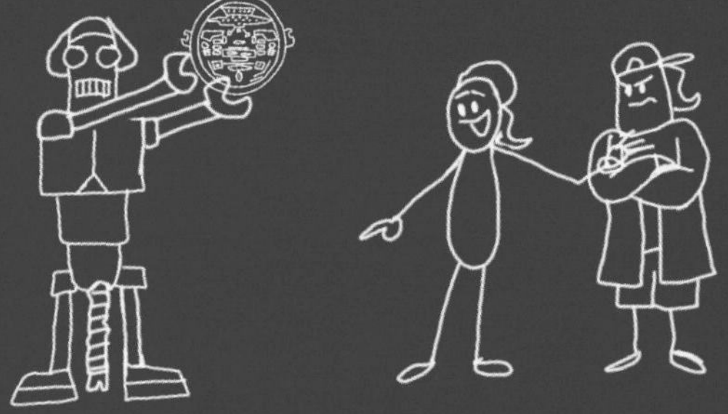

Figure E

He rejects the Doctor, proving his artificial intelligence has evolved to the point that it can think like a human

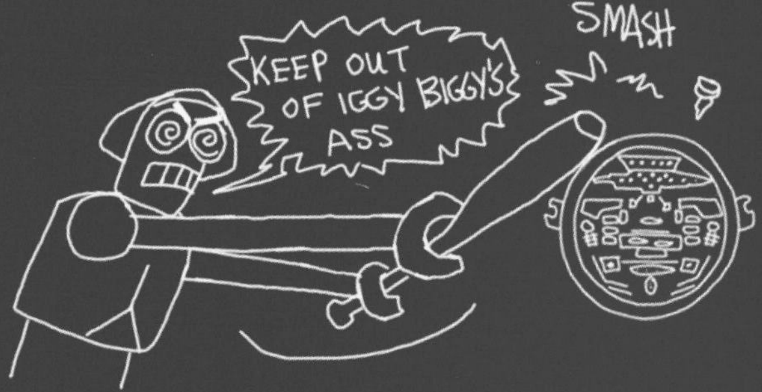
SMASH
KEEP OUT OF IGGY BIGGY'S ASS

Figure F

Realizing the danger, Jay and Bob stop Skynet from happening

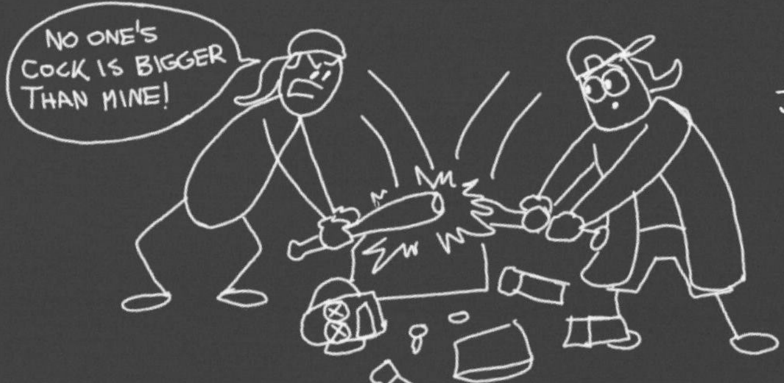
NO ONE'S COCK IS BIGGER THAN MINE!

OPERATION: DESTROY THE DICKHOLE ON THE VOLLEYBALL TEAM

Figure A

Join the volleyball fun league

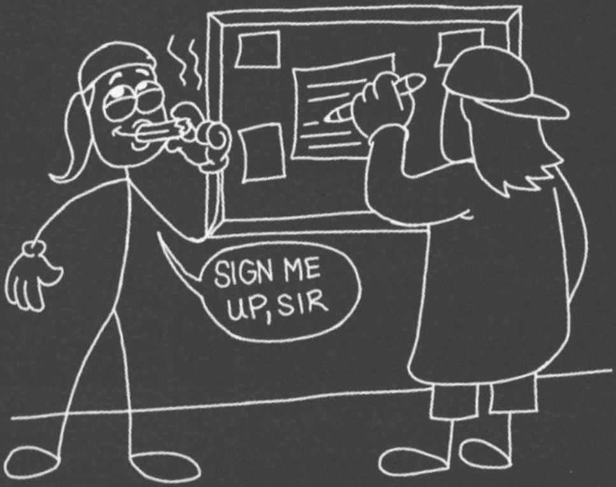
SIGN ME UP, SIR

Figure B

Have a miserable dickhole scoff at the team's every fault

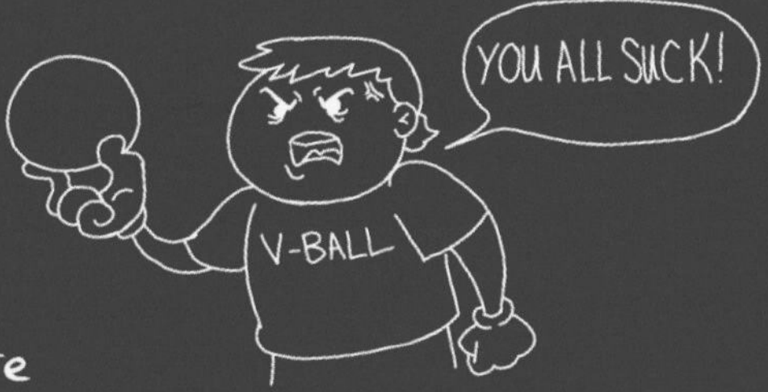
YOU ALL SUCK!
V-BALL

Figure C

Tell the other really competitive douche on the other team that he called him a fuckhole

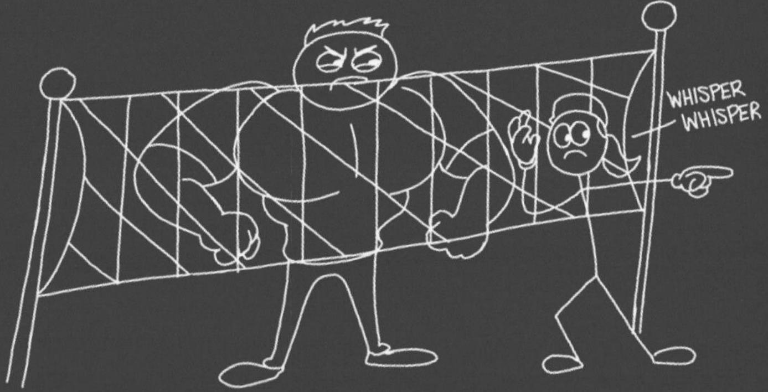
WHISPER WHISPER

Figure D

The dickhole gets spiked with the volleyball.
One competitor is carried off the court
and the other is escorted out

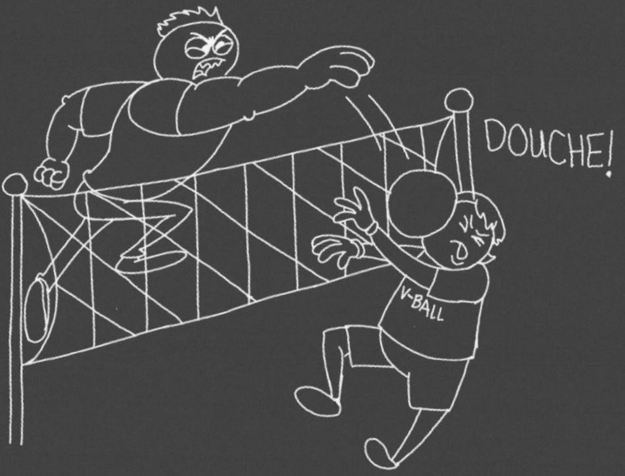
DOUCHE!
V-BALL

Figure E

Jay and Bob can finally
play with their balls in
peace and quiet

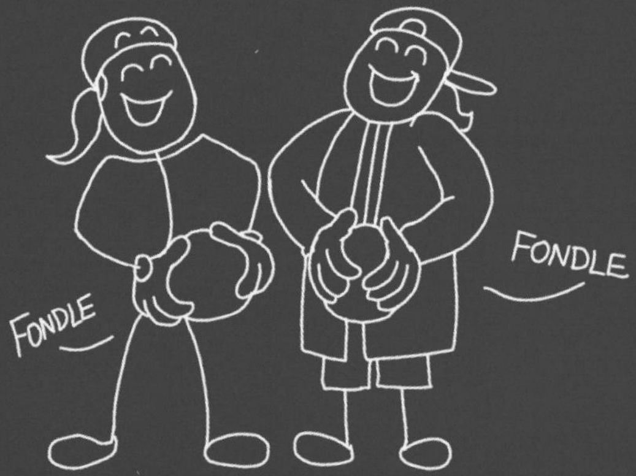
FONDLE
FONDLE

OPERATION: DESTROY BOYFRIEND WHO WANTS ANAL

Figure A

Get boyfriend to splurge on a fancy dinner with the promise of some butt-fucking

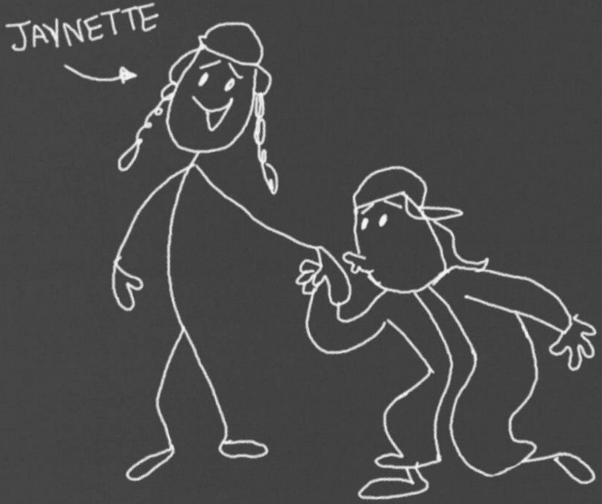
JAYNETTE

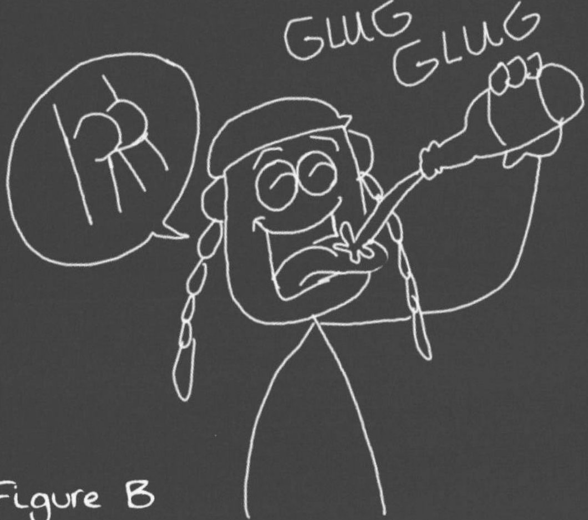
GLUG GLUG

Figure B

Eat and drink expensive food and booze while talking up how great butt-fucking is

Figure C Get boyfriend good and liquored-up so he can butt-fuck

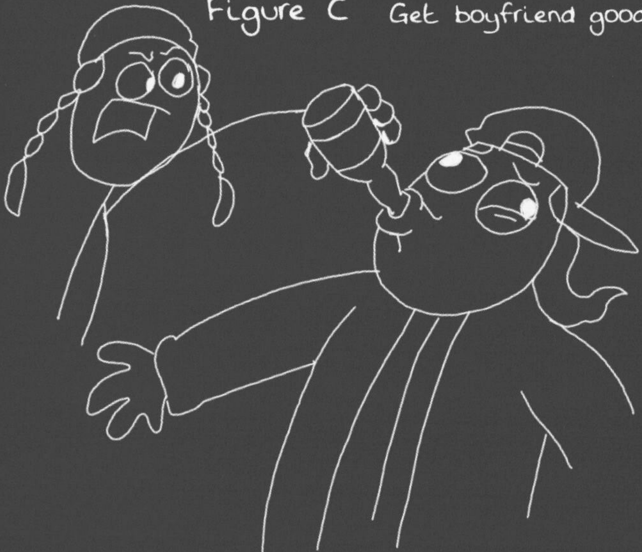

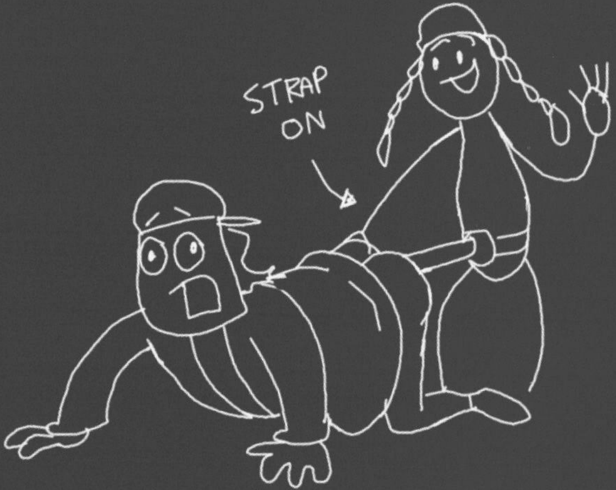
STRAP ON

Figure D Give him the butt-fucking he's always asking about

OPERATION: DESTROY AGORAPHOBIA

Figure A

This dude Jay and Bob know doesn't leave his house

OPEN UP, ASSHOLE! YOU HAVE OUR COPY OF MURDER SHE WROTE!

Figure B

Observe him not responding to out-of-doors stimuli

Figure C Get his garden hose

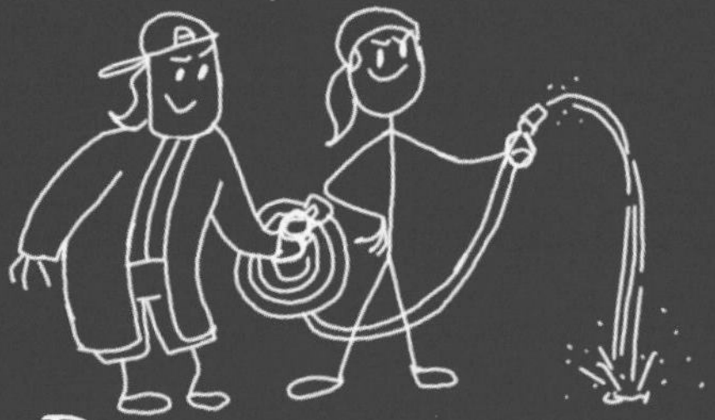

Figure D

Turn it on and fill his house up through his window

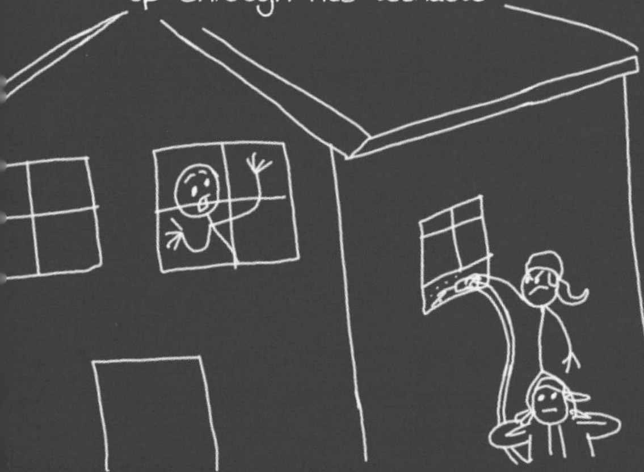

Figure E

Get back DVD, and that wussy turd sees the outdoors again

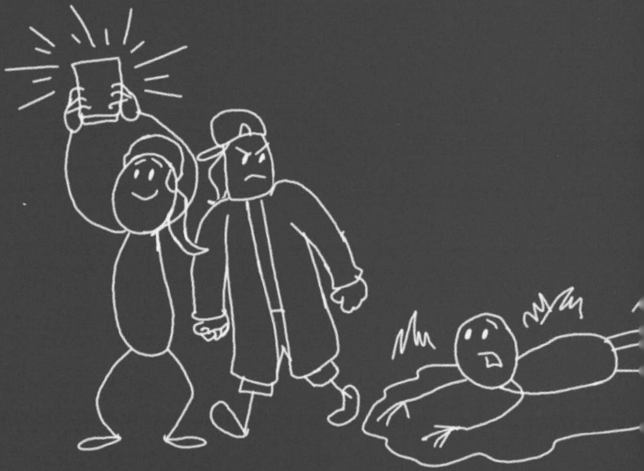

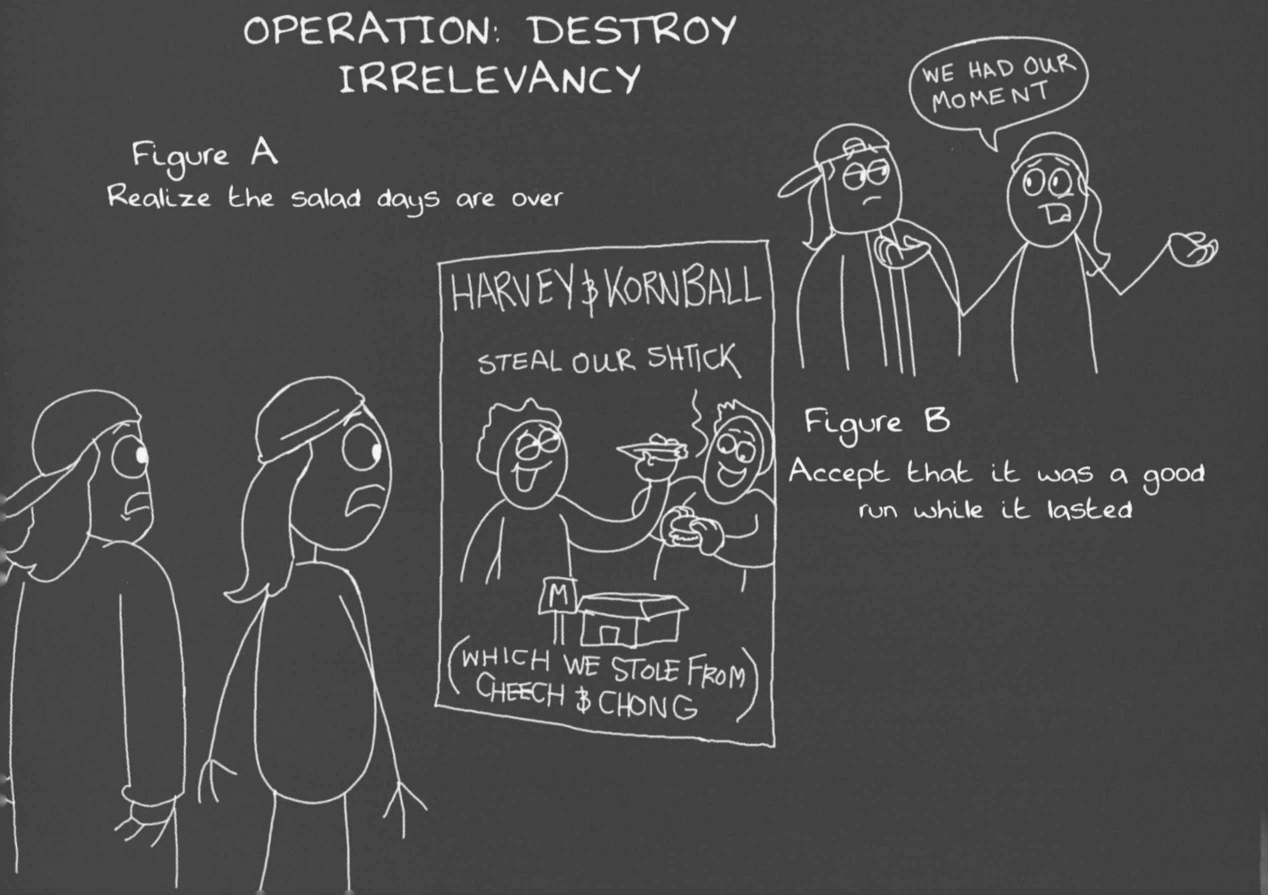
OPERATION: DESTROY IRRELEVANCY
Figure A
Realize the salad days are over
HARVEY $ KORNBALL
STEAL OUR SHTICK
M
(WHICH WE STOLE FROM CHEECH $ CHONG)
WE HAD OUR MOMENT
Figure B
Accept that it was a good run while it lasted

Realize this means getting actual jobs in the real world

Figure C

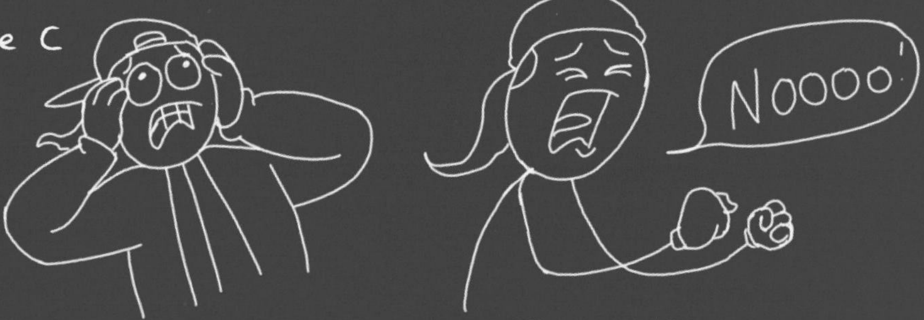
NOOOO!

Figure D

Re-label old shit as "classic" and embrace new technologies

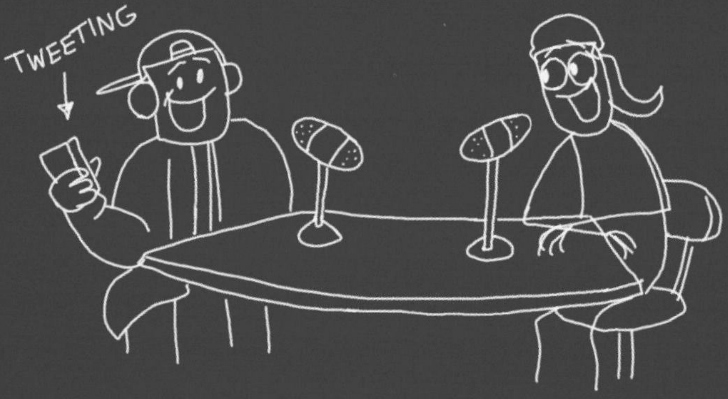
TWEETING

Figure E

Jay and Bob just bought themselves another fifteen minutes!

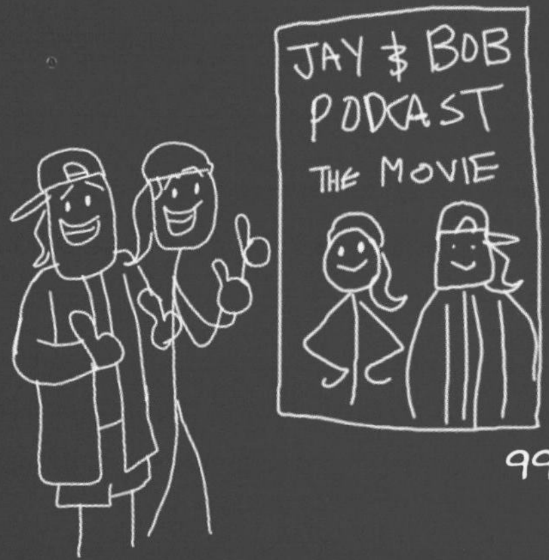
JAY $ BOB
PODCAST
THE MOVIE

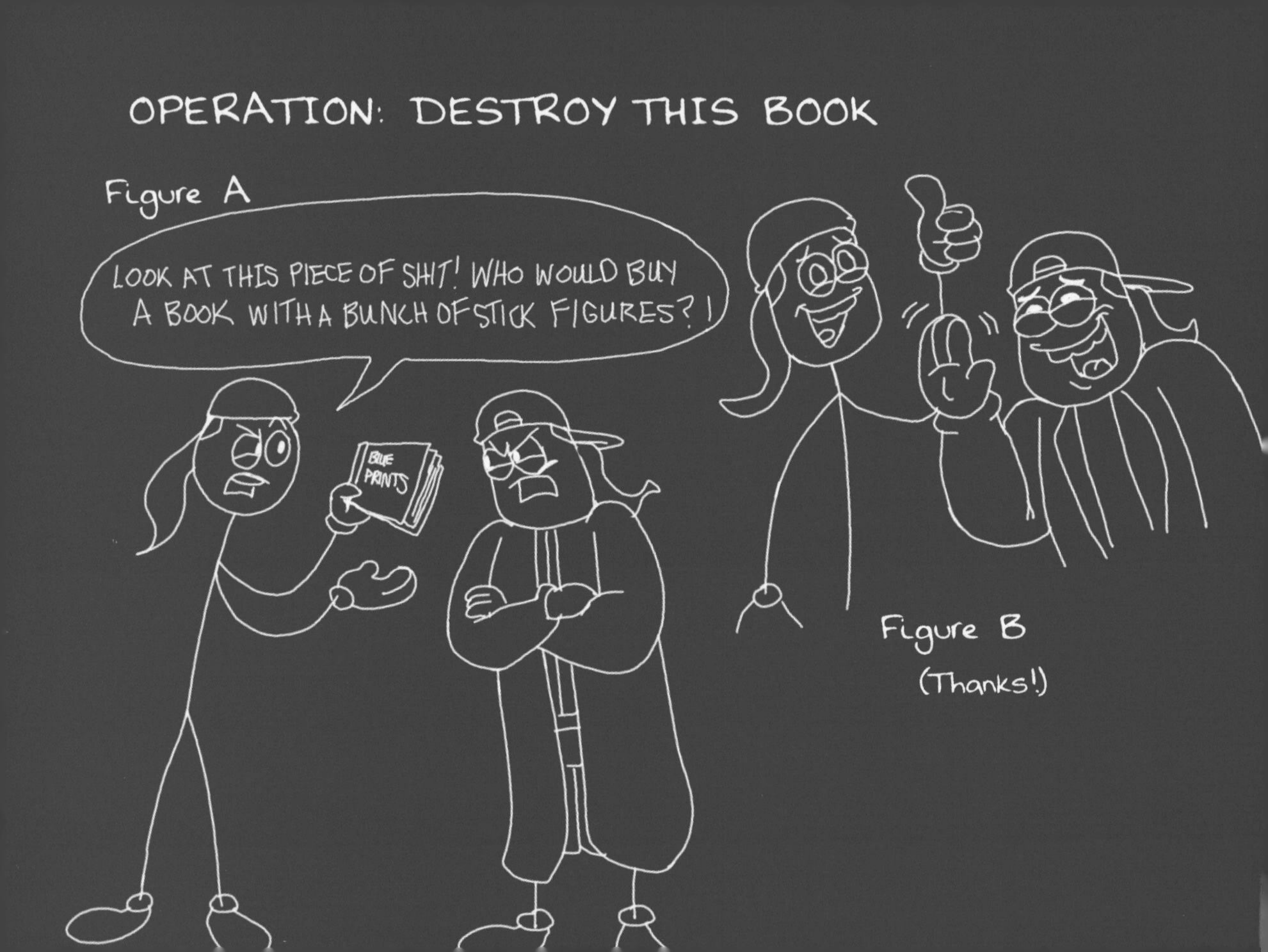
OPERATION: DESTROY THIS BOOK
Figure A
LOOK AT THIS PIECE OF SHIT! WHO WOULD BUY A BOOK WITH A BUNCH OF STICK FIGURES?!
BLUE PRINTS
Figure B
(Thanks!)

Figure C

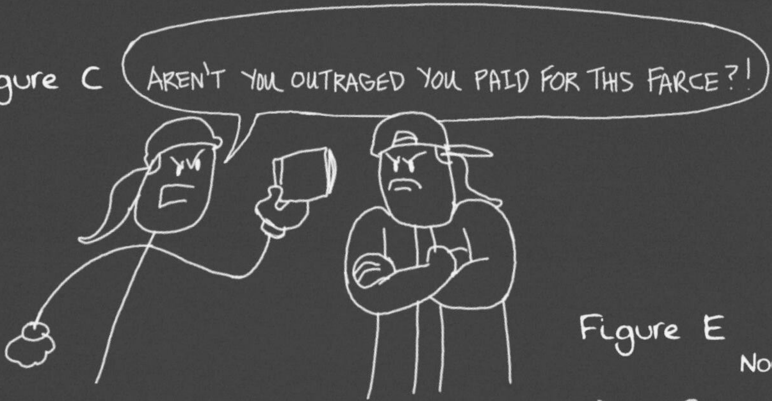
AREN'T YOU OUTRAGED YOU PAID FOR THIS FARCE?!

Figure D

Rip it to shreds!

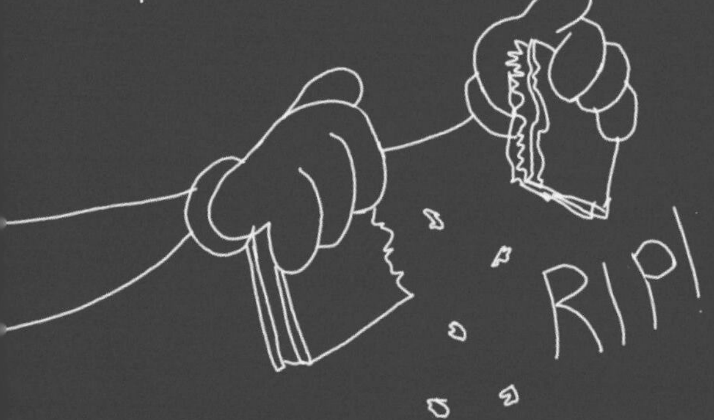
RIP!

Figure E

Now go buy another one!

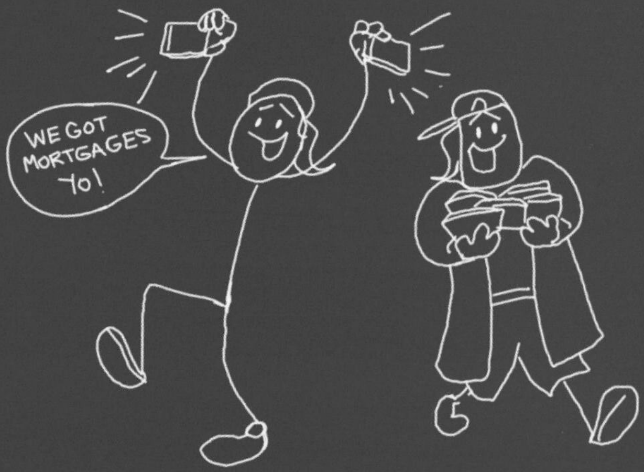
WE GOT MORTGAGES YO!

About the Authors

JASON MEWES is a television and film actor and producer best known for playing Jay, the vocal half of the Jay and Silent Bob duo in six films and an animated series. He currently cohosts a weekly podcast with Kevin Smith called *Jay and Silent Bob Get Old.*

KEVIN SMITH is a screenwriter, actor, film producer, and director, as well as a *New York Times* bestselling author, comic book writer, comedian/raconteur, and Internet radio personality best recognized by viewers as Silent Bob. He has directed movies such as *Clerks, Mallrats, Dogma,* and *Chasing Amy* and written four previous books and numerous comic books. He currently hosts the comedy podcast *SModcast*, the Hulu show *Spoilers,* and the AMC show *Comic Book Men.*

About the Artist

STEVE SARK is a man with a face and hair. He has been drawing since he was a sperm. He currently resides in Toronto with his wife and soon-to-be baby. Visit him at StarkToons.com.